Y0-BOY-931

The German Triangle
Carl Messinger

Copyright © 2020 Carl Messinger

All rights reserved. No part of this book may be reproduced or transmitted in any form or by any means, electronic or mechanical, including photocopying, recording or by any information storage and retrieval system without permission in writing from the publisher.

Imprint—JKL Publishing, Scottsdale, AZ.
ISBN: 978-0-578-67520-6
Library of Congress Control Number: 2020906769
Title: The German Triangle
Author: Carl Messinger
Digital distribution | 2020
Paperback | 2020

This is a work of fiction. The characters, names, incidents, places, and dialogue are products of the author's imagination, and are not to be construed as real.

Dedication

In this time of COVID-19, it is impossible to dedicate any menial endeavor such as this book to anyone other than those who struggle, strive, reach out, and perform their duties above and beyond what could be expected in the sometimes futile attempt to save a human life. A mere "thank you" is insufficient to sooth the pain of watching someone die, insufficient to watch the crying and weeping as loved ones pass on, and insufficient to realize that they have to go through it again, and again, and again.

A crippled man was once challenged to walk around a conference table without the aid of his crutches. He accepted the challenge and after two steps, fell to the floor. He got up, walked another two or three steps, and fell again. This continued many times until he had circled the table and returned to his seat. His colleagues were amazed that he had failed many times yet had still reached his destination.

When confronted with the fact that he had fallen, had failed so many times, his reply was simple.

"Failure is not the falling down, failure is not getting back up"

With the confidence and attitude of those who lead us in this terrible time,

WE WILL GET UP!

Chapter One

The cold damp fog hung over the landing field like a blanket struggling to keep a child warm. It swirled and moved as the wind shifted first one direction then another, unsure of its path, but knowing that it must keep moving. The fog had been there most of the night and the dawn had not yet gathered enough strength to chase it away. It enjoyed the last of its playtime without pondering the consequences of the appearance of the life-giving orb which would eventually probe through the mist and tear it into little shreds, shreds that would soon be nothing more than a memory of the night before and the vision of the night to come.

The dark form of the plane slowly rolled through the mist, escaping its cover as it crept down the taxiway toward the west end of the runway. High atop the concrete tower, a single pair of eyes tried to penetrate the watery darkness, hearing the noise of the engines way before actually seeing it. As the throbbing of the engines grew louder, the sleek silhouette form of the C-47 slowly emerged from the mist and moved purposefully in front of the tower. The watchful eyes could see the shadows of the men inside the cockpit going through their pre-flight check, something they had done many times before but something which they knew had to be done each time to enhance the possibility of a successful and safe flight.

Three men sat in the cockpit of the C-47. The pilot, in the left seat, was intense in his scrutiny of the instruments monitoring the health of the two Pratt and Whitney engines. His eyes flicked over the range of dials, registering in his mind their condition and comparing them to what he knew to be acceptable. One gauge, the oil pressure for the number one engine, seemed a little low and he reached out and flicked the glass dome, hoping to cause an adjustment of the tiny needle. After three flicks he resorted to a sharp whack with his closed fist. The tiny gauge jumped, and the needle, knowing it was beaten, moved further into the green and settled there. The co-pilot glanced over and chuckled.

The navigator, sitting behind the co-pilot, was buried in a map on the small ledge that served as a table. A tiny red lamp provided the illumination and combined with the white lights up front, formed an eerie shade of pink. With a ruler and protractor, he traced the proposed route onto the map, jotting down times, speeds, and locations as he figured out the best way to their destination. Emergency landing fields were identified and marked on the map and on the flight plan. Of course, there were no emergency landing fields in the English Channel and the navigator knew that once over the water their best course was to keep boring through the night sky till they reached the shores of France. He thought of the cold channel water and quickly turned back to his maps looking for the fastest way across the Channel.

The co-pilot had just about finished his check-list. He too had confirmed the normality of the engine gauges and had also checked the onboard fire extinguishing system, the transponder, and the radios. All seemed ready and he turned to the navigator and gave a thumbs up. The navigator returned the salute and they both looked at the pilot. As the plane moved into the mist away from the tower, the watchful eyes saw the pilot nod in acknowledgment. Another one was ready to go.

Reaching the end of the taxiway, the pilot rotated the wheel to the left, eased up on the throttle, and coasted the metal bird to a stop just before the runway. He made a final adjustment to his shoulder harness as the co-pilot strained to see through the fog to his right, hoping not to see the on-rushing lights of a plane landing. The navigator glanced nervously around well aware that if something was going to happen, the chances are that it would happen at take-off or landing. His eyes fell on the escape hatch and he mentally opened it and climbed out of the burning wreckage to safety. His concern was interrupted by the status of the radio relaying instructions from the watchful eyes in the tower.

"Roger, C-87463, you are cleared for runway 090."

Without a word, the pilot slowly eased the throttles forward and the props of the two engines ground into the misty air, slowly pulling the plane onto the runway. The white line marking the center of the concrete ribbon came into view and the nose of the plane slowly swung left, its uplifted profile pointing down the length of the ribbon, its tail wheel slightly to the left of perfect.

"Lakenheath tower, this is C-87463 ready for take-off."

"Roger, C-87463, you are cleared for take-off. Good luck."

The pilot slowly pushed the throttles forward while keeping his foot on the brake. The co-pilot reached over with his left hand and placed it behind the pilot's, a procedure meant to ensure that the pilot did not accidentally pull back on the throttles in a critical moment causing the plane to lose its forward momentum and crash into the very earth it was trying to leave.

The engines began to whine at a high pitch and the fuselage of the plane started to shake as the metal bird strained at the bit, eager to rid itself of its earthly status and assume its rightful position in the sky. The pilot and co-pilot watched the gauges until satisfied that both engines had achieved sufficient RPM. With a sudden jolt that threw the co-pilot and navigator against their harnesses, the pilot released the pressure from the brake and the anxious bird began to run to the sky.

Runways are never as smooth as they look, and it took considerable skill and strength to keep the plane in a straight line. The pilot, one hand on the throttles and one hand on the wheel, glanced back and forth from the air speed indicator to the runway, then back to the air speed indicator. The co-pilot, his hand still resting behind the throttle, called out the air speed over the intercom to assist the pilot. The navigator just sat there, his fingers tightly gripping the arms of his chair, his eyes closed and his mind praying.

About a third of the way down the runway, almost opposite the tower, the tail wheel lifted off the concrete. Immediately, the vibration of the plane was considerably lessened. Only the two wing wheels now kept the plane out of its natural element. Passing before the tower, the pilot could feel the charging plane begin to feel the lift, as the wheels now bounced more than rolled. As the air speed indicator passed the critical point, the pilot eased back on the wheel and the well named Gooney Bird left the confines of the ground and gracefully rose into the sky, its lights blinking a farewell to the still watchful eyes in the tower.

It was February, 1948 and Air Force Lieutenant Ron Matthews was en route to occupied Germany. It was his first trip to the war-ravished country having joined the effort to free the world of the Nazi terror too late to have any impact. After graduating from college in New Jersey he joined the Army as did many others before him, and reported to Fort Dix for basic training. While there, he applied for flight training and six weeks later found himself at flight school in Alabama. He had enjoyed flight school, at least the second half of it. The first half of the course had been spent in the classroom learning the theory of flight, flight procedures, tactics, and all the other things one had to learn to be able to stay alive in the air. Having just spent four years behind the desk, he was yearning for something more exciting and eager to get into the air.

The second half of flight school was tough, but exciting for Matthews. He was eager to prove himself and spent every available moment on the flight line

5

talking with the maintenance chiefs and mechanics to learn as much as possible about the planes. While his fellow students hurriedly rushed to see the many young ladies anxious to meet an Army pilot, Matthews climbed in, around, and under the different aircraft to learn how and why they flew. He became familiar with weapons systems on fighters, with bomb-bays on the bigger bombers. He traced wiring for radios and intercoms and fuel lines leading from the fuel tanks to the engines. He studied schematics with the crew chiefs to troubleshoot problems and served as a go-fer just to be able to watch the mechanic fix the problem. Initially considered a pain by the maintenance crews, he had earned their respect by his sincere desire to learn their trade. By the end of flight school, he either knew how to fix a problem, or knew where to go to get the answer to the problem.

But his true love was being in the air. The first time in a plane he was like a kid in a candy store. His instructor had to keep on reminding him that this was just an orientation flight, a chance for him to get accustomed to being off the ground. Matthews wanted to stay up forever, soaring over the countryside. He constantly looked down at the ground below, knowing that flying was the one thing he wanted to do in his life. He loved the feeling of flight, of being with the birds. He enjoyed the freedom from the routine of gravity, the control of his own destiny as he skillfully guided the trainer for the first time. The first flight had ended all too soon, but what he had experienced would stay with him for the rest of his life.

The steady drone of the two Pratt and Whitney R-1830-92 engines sounded like sweet music to Matthews' ears as he skillfully steered the C-47 through the mist and the clouds toward the East, the light of the rising sun beginning to show itself and shove aside the darkness. He glanced over the instruments and found everything to be satisfactory. His co-pilot was performing lookout duties, peering out the still fog-surrounded windows in what would have been a vain effort if in fact he did sight another plane approaching. The navigator had loosened his grip on his chair and was intently trying to determine their location using an average speed, along with his watch, and the compass nestled among the other instruments between the two men in front of him.

The combined 2,400 horsepower of the two engines smoothly pulled them upward toward the lightening sky. The gray mist started to grow thinner and thinner, flecks of dark blue beginning to punctuate the sky like the blue crystals in laundry soap. The crystals multiplied rapidly and the combination of the falling ground and the rising sun soon provided an azure blue carpet upon which the outstretched wings of the C-47 seemed to rest.

Reaching an altitude of 16,000 feet, Matthews gently tilted the nose of the plane down until they were flying level. A check of the airspeed indicator showed 190 miles per hour, about 40 miles below the plane's maximum speed. The heading was almost due East. The navigator tried to visually check his location but the fog below hampered his attempt. The next major landmark would be the English Channel, so he would have to wait till then. All indicators were normal so Matthews handed the controls over to his co-pilot, squeezed past the navigator and entered the cargo compartment of the plane.

For the most part the cargo compartment was empty. His duffel and those of the other two crewmen lay on the floor near the door. A couple of canvas bags containing mail were strewn alongside them. The canvas web seats were strapped to the bulkheads. When dropped into place, they held 28 troops with full equipment. Matthews had only seen a full compartment one time. It had been back in the States when he was transitioning from a single engine aircraft to dual engine. Part of the transition was taking part in war games and he was assigned to transport troops to a dirt strip somewhere in Georgia. He remembered being concerned about the troops' safety, their lives being dependent on his flying skills. He was glad he did not have to do it in combat.

Matthews started to go through his duffel but was stopped by the compartment speaker crackling that the Channel was in sight. He stood up and walked back to the cockpit, again squeezing past the navigator who seemed pleased with himself because their actual location closely corresponded with where he had calculated them to be.

Matthews climbed back into his seat, adjusted his shoulder harness and looked through the narrow window of the steady plane. The jagged coastline of England was rapidly approaching and he could easily make out where the land ended and the water began. Scattered boats up and down the coast bounded on the often-white waves as their crews sought to make a living by reaping what the sea had to offer. This was not as easy as it seemed to be as the currents of the North Sea meet those of the Atlantic Ocean and often caused rough seas. Combine that with the strong winds, and Matthews knew the idyllic setting he watched pass under his plane was more in the mind than in reality.

Matthews remembered his history and the role of the English Channel as a protector of England from invasion. Before Hitler's failure to cross the Channel, others like the Spanish Armada and Napoleon's fleet had tried and failed. The advent of the airplane had removed the invincibility of the Channel as the supreme protector of England. That role had been taken over by the RAF. But the Channel still did its job as a deterrent to invasion. Not since William, Duke of Normandy, invaded England and defeated the English at the Battle of Hastings in October, 1066 had the Channel failed in its duty to turn away a land invasion.

Out the left window, Matthews could see the town of Dover sliding behind the wing. The legendary white cliffs of Dover consisting of chalk and limestone also came and went. Their flight across the channel was planned to be over the narrowest part, a mere 21 miles wide. At their current air speed the crossing would take just under seven minutes. Already he could see the French coast dead ahead and the small town he knew to be Calais.

Matthews glanced over to his co-pilot and motioned that he would take over the duties. He loved to fly and while he knew he had to let his co-pilot have some air time, he would have flown the whole way had it been up to him. The flight from Calais to just outside of Frankfurt was about 400 miles. He would fly the first 100 miles, then let his co-pilot take it till they contacted Rhein-Main Air Base. He would take it in from there.

His intercom crackled and the navigator advised Matthews to head a little south, just a couple of degrees, but it would put them on the right path to their destination without having to make any last minute adjustments. Turning slightly south, they flew over the Belgium countryside, over its capital, Brussels, and then over Luxembourg. Matthews recognized what once had been one of Europe's strongest fortresses high above the Alzette River. Started in 963 as a small castle, it had grown and developed into a mighty structure situated along important trade routes. In May of 1940, it fell to the Nazi troops in one day.

Matthews heard the navigator issue instructions to the co-pilot to change his direction and felt the plane turn a little to the left and straighten out. They were over Germany now and not far from Rhein-Main. He reached down and picked up the flight plan and looked for the new radio setting. The gauge on the instrument panel had not been changed and he glanced back over his right shoulder to see what the navigator was doing. The navigator was just checking his plan and he reached up to switch the frequency to the proper channel. Matthews clicked on his radio and spoke.

"Rhein-Main tower, this is C-87463. Come in please."

"Roger, C-87463, this is Rhein-Main tower. We have you on the screen at 75 miles west. Begin your descent on my command."

"Roger, waiting.

Matthews glanced at his co-pilot and took over the controls of the aircraft. As he approached the airfield, he and the tower kept up a steady dialogue, one directing, the other flying. The airfield was about 20 miles away and Matthews could make out its racetrack shape. The main runaway was flanked by a taxiway on either side. The taxiway met at each end of the runway forming a large oval with the runway bisecting the oval length-wise. The area surrounding it had been stripped bare of vegetation and the whole airfield looked like it was some sort of alien carving meant to give directions. Matthews sighed and turned the plane onto its final approach.

The rubber tires hit the pavement with a screech before they caught the friction and started to rotate. Matthews immediately reduced the throttle and allowed the craft to steady itself before applying a light touch to the brakes. He had learned that an initial light touch was necessary to ensure that both wheels were braking evenly. All too often, one brake would grab more severely than the other and the pilot had to wrestle the craft back to a straight line. Sometimes they were not successful with the result that the airplane swerved off the runway onto the dirt and airplanes don't do well on dirt. Several such instances had etched into his mind the need for a light touch.

As the plane slowed down in a straight line, Matthews applied more pressure to the brakes and reversed the pitch of the propellers. This reversing allowed the engines to slow down the plane and reduced the possibility of burning out the brakes. He knew that maintenance people did not like replacing brakes on airplanes. It made them seem more like a garage-monkey than a mechanic. Matthews smiled as he thought that keeping his mechanics happy was a good thing.

A jeep pulled out from the side of the runway and moved in front of the C-47. The passenger waved to follow him and the tiny convoy moved to the taxiway, then to a line of other C-47's, their noses turned up and facing the runway. The jeep turned to go behind them and Matthews followed like a puppy looking for dinner. Making a sharp right, the jeep moved through an unoccupied spot between two aircraft. The passenger waved as a crew chief stepped in front to guide the plane to a stop. Two personnel, one on each side, stood waiting with wooden chocks to place at the wheels when the plane stopped.

Matthews slowly inched his craft forward, watching the signals from the crew chief. As the plane neared its resting place, the guide moved his hands closer together over his head until finally the hands clasped. Matthews applied the final little touch to the brakes, and the plane settled into its new home. The wheel chocks were put into place and the crew chief signaled to kill the engines.

The pilots quickly went through their final checklist as the navigator shed his harness and moved to the rear of the plane to open the door. One of the ground crew was waiting to assist with the steps and to help with whatever cargo had just arrived. The navigator handed out the bags of mail, looked around to make sure there was nothing else, then handed out the duffel bags for the crew. He glanced toward the cockpit and saw the two pilots headed in his direction. Without a word, he stepped out the door, down the steps and onto the concrete. Matthews and the co-pilot followed behind him.

"Sergeant McKensie, Sir, welcome to Rhein-Main," the ground guide said as he saluted the officers.

Matthews returned the salute and shook the sergeant's hand.

"Thank you, Sergeant, great to be here."

Sergeant McKensie motioned to a jeep waiting nearby and the driver moved to the group of men. The ground crew threw the duffels in the back of the vehicle, leaving just enough room for the navigator and the co-pilot. Matthews climbed into the front seat and the driver started rolling past the line of planes toward the operations building. Once inside, they signed in, handed over their personnel files and were assigned a place to stay.

"Lieutenant Matthews," the clerk said, "we have found a small apartment in a town just south of here. It is just a temporary thing until we get more billets built here on base. There is a jeep to take you there now and one will pick you up tomorrow morning at 0700 hours."

Matthews said good-bye to his co-pilot and navigator and said he would see them in the morning. The jeep was where the clerk said it would be and the driver saluted and helped with the duffel bag. Matthews climbed into the front seat and they smoothly pulled away from the operations building. About a mile or so, they passed through the gate, the guards snapping to attention and saluting smartly. Matthews returned their salute and settled deeper into the seat to avoid the chilly February air. While there was no snow on the ground, the wind was cold, as Frankfurt and Rhein-Main were about the same latitude as the southern tip of the Hudson Bay in Canada.

The jeep traveled quickly through the countryside, slowing or stopping only at intersections to ensure a safe passage. About fifteen minutes later, a little sign next to the road announced their arrival at the town of Oberstdorf, a small village with cobble streets, clean sidewalks and what looked like one or two main streets. The driver turned right and pulled up in front of a stone house, its windows covered with wooden slats or blinds and no sign of life. The driver shut off the engine, hopped out and grabbed the duffel bag. Matthews climbed out of the jeep and walked the three steps to the door. Seeing no button, he knocked on the door to get someone's attention. A tiny round opening in the door opened to reveal an eye peeking out from inside. Immediately, the opening closed and Matthews could hear locks being turned. The door opened and an elderly German woman stood smiling.

Frau Schlegal was close to seventy. She stood about five feet tall, had gray hair which was pulled back into a bun. Her dress, while not new, was clean and neat. Her face reflected the hardships she had endured, the wrinkles effectively covering the beauty that had once been there. But her eyes gave it away. They were expressive, bright, a little child's eyes, big

14

with wonderment, smothered with excitement. Matthews realized that they were eyes that someone could easily fall in love with. Now if she was only twenty years old, he thought, laughing to himself.

With broken English, she welcomed him and led him upstairs to show him his appointed room. The driver followed, carrying the duffel. The room was small, but clean and cozy. A big window looked out the back of the house to several hills covered with vineyards, or at least what had once been vineyards. They were mostly barren, but he could see that work had begun to restore them to their former condition. The bed was a double, covered with a huge eiderdown, a quilt stuffed with duck feathers. A small chest stood opposite the bed, a mirror above it, and a washbowl and pitcher on it. A small towel rack on the side of the chest held a clean towel. What looked to be an armoire stood up against a second wall. Seeing no closets, Matthews opened the armoire and found two hangers in it. He closed the doors and looked for the bathroom.

"There doesn't appear to be one," the driver said. He turned and said to the woman, "Toiletten?"

She smiled and pointed down the hall. They walked down the hall and opened the door at the end. A small tub with a shower head held sway of the far end of the room. A commode, the water tank attached to the wall above the fixture, stood guard. A sink finished the contents of the room. Everything seemed clean and neatly kept. Matthews smiled at Frau Schlegal and uttered his first German word.

"Gut," he said.

She smiled and turned and walked back down the hall and down the steps. Matthews confirmed that he would be picked up tomorrow morning, thanked the driver for his help, and dismissed him. He then went about the business of unpacking his few belongings.

Ten minutes later, he walked downstairs and found Frau Schlegal sitting in what must have been the living room, a nice fire in the fireplace, sipping a cup of tea and reading a book. He knocked on the door to get her attention, waiting for her invitation before entering the room. She looked up and motioned for him to enter.

Hesitantly, he took a couple of steps into the room, then brought his hand to his mouth like he was eating, or wanting to eat. She smiled and got up from her chair and walked to the front door. She opened the door and said something in German. Matthews did not understand.

"Zum Rose," she said again, pointing down the street. "Essen, Essen," she repeated.

Matthews now understood "Essen," smiled and stared out the door. Before he could get through and outside, she tapped him on the arm. He turned to look at her. She reached into the pocket of her apron and took out a key, apparently a key to the front door. Matthews looked at the key, then at Frau Schlegal.

"Danke," he said softly, bowing slightly.

Frau Schlegal smiled, nodded her head, then stepped inside and closed the door. Matthews looked at the key, found the house number for later use, then turned and walked down the street in the direction that his new landlady had pointed.

16

"This is going to be ok," he thought as he looked for the zum Rose.

Chapter Two

Matthews walked quickly down the street, the building on his right acting like a railing to keep him on the straight and narrow. The sidewalk was clean of debris, but cracked in places still waiting to be repaired. It appeared the town had not been severely damaged from the constant bombing by the Allies, or what damage had been done had already been removed from sight and taken away. The ancient cobblestone road showed freshly repaired patches. The new sections contrasted sharply with those which had witnessed the passing of hundreds of years and he wondered if they could talk, would they speak of the passing of Roman soldiers, or perhaps the legions of Charles the Great, whose ancient capital of the Holy Roman Empire was less than one hundred and fifty miles away. He had heard about Aachen and would have to take a trip there sometime.

In sharp contrast to American neighborhood streets, Oberstdorf's streets were void of people. The front windows of all the houses were covered with wooden shutters which appeared to be able to be rolled up when desired, exposing the window and thus the inside, to outside conditions. Across the street from the houses a gently sloping hill rose from the street, its incline neatly sliced by rows of grape vines now dormant for the winter. Narrow walkways between the rows allowed for grape pickers to quickly go through their task of collecting the grapes and bringing them back for processing. Matthews thought that would be a back-breaking job and wondered exactly how it was done without winding up crippled.

The rows of vines rose up the hill and pointed to the ruins of a castle at its top. The castle was small, probably no more than a lookout post used hundreds of years before, and he doubted that anyone had ever lived there. Two of the walls were almost completely gone, and a third was partially destroyed. The single tower rose majestically into the sky, but it too was incomplete, having suffered at the hands of time. He wondered if, like American kids playing cowboys and Indians, the German kids played Roman Soldiers and Germanic tribes. He chuckled at his poor attempt at humor.

He reached the corner of the block and was about to cross over when he heard a door being opened in the building to his right. He stopped for a minute, thinking of asking whoever it was the location of the restaurant. Two elderly German men came out of the door. They spotted him and stopped and stared. One turned and said something to the other, who nodded his head in reply. Without another word they let the door close behind them, turned right and slowly moved away

As Matthews looked at the door, hoping that someone else would exit, he noticed a larger than usual stone set into the wall next to the door. Etched in small letters and barely discernible were the words "zum Rose." No other sign or notice gave proof to what was inside the door and he felt thankful for his landlady who had told him about the name of the restaurant and where to find it. Otherwise, he thought, he would still be walking.

The heavy and thick outside door opened easily and Matthews found himself in a small anteroom, a second door straight ahead with thick glass windows allowing him to see inside. He went to reach for the second door and found that he had to release the handle of the outside door before he could do it. As he let go of the outside door, it smoothly returned to its closed posture and clicked as it settled into position. Matthews reasoned that the double door kept out the cold air, and the distance between the doors was set so that both could not be opened by the same person at the same time. An effective means of keeping the cold out and the heat in.

The restaurant was not very large. About six wooden tables stood scattered around the wooden floor, their tops covered with tablecloths of various designs and sizes. Four booths lined the wall to his right and a small bar, probably just for the waitress lined the wall on his left. A couple of stools stood at attention in front of the bar, but they appeared to be there just for show as the bar area in front of them was crowded with a variety of objects to include plants, glasses and dishes. A single wooden rail, once the object of tired feet, stood about eight inches above the floor and ringed the bottom of the bar.

The place was empty except for two other American pilots sitting at one of the tables in the middle of the floor. They glanced up from their salads as he entered, and he nodded and moved to their table.

"Hi, Ron Matthews," he said, introducing himself and stretching out a hand.

"Hello," said the closest American grabbing Matthews' hand. "Tom Reynolds."

"Jim Wistick, how are you?" said the second American.

"Doing well, thank you. Just got into Rhein-Main this afternoon and S-1 put me up in a room up the street till something on base came available. Haven't eaten since breakfast and the landlady recommended this place."

The two Americans laughed and looked at each other.

"This is the only place in town," said the one who had introduced himself as Tom Reynolds. "But it's pretty good, close, and since you'll be on separate rations for a while, the cost is definitely right. Just hope you like veal, because beef is hard to come by outside of the mess hall. Grab a seat."

Matthews pulled out one of the two empty seats and sat down. He reached for a paper menu that lay on the table and scanned its offering. Most of the items he could not understand. Some, like Salat and Beire, he reasoned. Others he had no idea what they were. He glanced over to Jim's plate.

"Wiener Schnitzel, breaded veal cutlet," said Jim, his mouth full of food.

Tom motioned for somebody to come to the table and Matthews turned to see who it was. An older man had come out of the kitchen and stopped behind the bar. Upon being beckoned, he came toward them, limping very badly on his right leg. But he had a big smile on his face, and his eyes shone bright with anticipation of being able to serve. His clean but worn pants were covered with an apron containing two pockets. Sticking out of one appeared to be a bottle opener or some such apparatus. The other was filled with something Matthews could not make out.

Herr Kurtz was about 50 years old, give or take a hundred. His gray hair was beginning to recede and the wrinkles on his face made him seem older than he really was, or anyone should be. The gray in his hair was matched by the gray in his eyebrows, and his puffed out cheeks, reddened by a little too much Jagermeister, gave him the appearance of a chipmunk well into his winter storage of nuts. Most noticeably, his right leg seemed unable to function to any great degree. While it provided support when standing still, it was an impediment to his walking. He tried to make light of it but it was obvious that there was some pain.

"Herr Kurtz, this is Ron Matthews. He is living up the street, probably Frau Schlegal's," Tom looked quizzically at the newcomer.

Matthews glanced at Reynolds and nodded in the affirmative. He reached his hand out to Herr Kurtz and the old German took it into his grizzled hands and shook it vigorously.

"Es freut mich," the old man said, his hand pumping up and down like a handle on a water pump, a broad smile on his face. He appeared genuinely happy to see the new American pilot.

Matthews returned the handshake. "Hello," he said, lowering his head a little in respect.

"Was wurst due," he said as he continued to pump Matthews' hand.

22

Matthews' face became blank and he looked at his new found colleagues for guidance. They laughed as they explained that he wanted to know what he would like to eat."

"Ya, Ya, Essen, Essen," said the innkeeper.

Matthews looked confused, thought quickly and then decided to rely on the age-old method of repetition. He pointed to the plate in front of Wistick, smiled, and said, "Das."

Herr Kurtz nodded in understanding, let go of Matthews' hand and turned to go away. The three Americans watched him drag his right leg across the floor and into the kitchen before resuming their conversation.

"What's with the leg?" Matthews asked the other two.

"Landmine," said Reynolds, "in France," resuming his eating.

"You mean we did that to him?" Matthews asked.

"Well," said Wistick, "yes and no." Matthews looked puzzled.

"It was an Allied mine," Wistick continued, "but it was WWI, not this one. He was wounded during the first couple days of the war and returned here to be with his wife. He understood he was one of the lucky ones in the village. Most did not return."

Matthews wanted to discuss more, but the others were busy eating. He decided to hold his questions to a more appropriate time. He could smell the aroma of food cooking coming out of the kitchen and hear the sizzling oil used in making the potatoes. As if by magic, a small salad appeared in front of him, and before he could turn and say thank you, Herr Kurtz had turned and headed back to the kitchen.

The salad was fresh, with vinegar and oil dressing scattered over the top. Additional dressing was in the cruets on the table. Conspicuous by their absence were tomatoes, winter not being the season. Instead, some red cabbage was mixed into the lettuce and that, along with both red and white onions, made a wonderful tasty salad. Matthews ate it with great vigor.

The hot steaming Wiener Schnitzel soon appeared with a pile of Pommes Frites, or French fries, as Matthews was soon to learn. Herr Kurtz stood to the side offering a bottle of beer with a smile on his face. Matthews glanced at the two other bottles on the table and nodded yes. With great flourish, Herr Kurtz grabbed the neck of the bottle and with his two thumbs on either side of the bottle, pushed the metal clasp away from his body. Immediately, the small porcelain top surrounded by an even smaller rubber grommet came loose. He put the bottle on the table, reached into his apron pocket and produced a glass. Taking a towel from his back pocket, he wiped and cleaned the glass before putting it down next to the bottle of beer. Matthews poured a little beer into the glass, took a sip, then dug into one of the best meals he had ever had.

All was quiet for the next fifteen minutes or so, until all had finished eating. The three Americans settled back into their seats and began to talk about the war, what they had done, and what they were going to do when they got back to the States. Both Reynolds and Wistick were fighter pilots. They had flown against the Luftwaffe for a better part of a year and had handled themselves with a great deal of distinction. While neither was an ace, they had both been credited with several kills. Matthews listened intently, not having anything to say that would compare with their stories.

The conversation soon turned to Nazism, how it got started and what it had done to the German people and how it had almost taken over the world. While they were discussing Hitler and his regime, Herr Kurtz came to clear the table. Though his English was not very good, he did understand when they used the word "Hitler" and "Nazi," and he stopped to listen to the discussion.

The discussion had gotten fairly animated and then Matthews was stunned when Herr Kurtz put the dishes down, stood up straight, and spit on the floor. He was astonished.

"Nazi," he said, and spit again, the hatred spewing from his mouth. He turned and walked away, a little straighter this time.

Matthews turned to the other Americans seated with him. "I don't understand," he said, looking for an explanation.

Reynolds started to explain. Herr Kurtz had volunteered for a German Army at a time when German honor and pride was thought to be at stake. He, and most of the other German population, looked at the worsening international situation at that time as a test of their strength, their inner strength, as a nation. They had grown to be one of the leading economic industrial countries in the world and desired to take their place among the world leaders.

Their enemy, if in fact there was one, was the outside world. And some say that they welcomed the opportunity to flex their muscles. What could have been a small scale war between Austria-Hungary and Serbia was allowed to escalate to a large war, enabling Germany to become a major player on the world scene. But all along, the German people were led to believe that the threat to their rightful place on the world scene was coming from outside the German borders. And in a frightful few days, Austria declared war on Serbia. Russia, Serbia's traditional ally declared war on Austria. Germany declared war on Russia, being Austria's ally. France, being allied with Russia, declared war on Germany. And Great Britain declared war on Germany, being allied with the French. The whole continent was allowed to become a fiery battleground.

The difference, at least as Herr Kurtz saw it, was that World War II and the conditions within Germany which led to the war, had been blamed on internal enemies of the state, specifically Jews and Bolsheviks. Hitler's propaganda machine accused these two groups of undermining Germany's struggle in WWI and causing Germany's loss, and with it, the loss of their sovereign rights as a free nation. His goal was to convince the German people that their loss earlier was the result of internal sedition leading to military defeat and that, as a result, 1) those two groups of people needed to be eliminated, and 2) the areas which had been unfairly taken away from Germany, unfairly because the other countries had been aided by the internal sedition, in other words it was not a fair war, should be returned to Germany.

Matthews listened intently. Reynolds continued on, relating a story about how one of Herr Kurtz's daughter's friends, a Jewish girl, had been rounded up one night taken away from the town, never to be heard from again. In fact, the whole family had been taken from their beds, thrown in a truck, and driven away. Herr Kurtz had known this family all his life and knew them to be loyal Germans. His personal knowledge of this family contrasted sharply with what was being said about the Jews and Bolsheviks. This single incident was enough to make him understand that the Nazis were not telling the truth and were just looking for scapegoats to unify the German populace and gain their support. It had worked and Herr Kurtz hated the Nazis for bringing the suffering to the German people.

Matthews and Wistick just sat there listening to Reynolds explain the reasoning behind Herr Kurtz's hatred of the Nazis. The sound of the outside door closing broke their concentration and they turned to look at who had entered the restaurant.

A young woman was taking off her scarf and coat and hung them up on a coat rack by the kitchen door.

"Ingrid," said Reynolds, "Herr Kurtz's daughter."

Ingrid was a slight girl, around 23 or 24 years old, with light colored hair, rosy cheeks, and a body that was trim and fit. The intensity in her eyes matched those of her father's and the freedom and lithe movement of her body mirrored what her father's movements must have been like before the landmine. She was an attractive woman who seemed to keep to herself and did not seem to have any boyfriends hanging around. She helped her father with the restaurant, and in fact, had just returned from the local Lebensmittel (grocery store) with a basket full of bread, rolls, cabbage, and onions. She glanced at the American pilots but said nothing.

Herr Kurtz came out of the kitchen door and smiled when he saw his daughter. Ingrid returned the smile and gave him a daughterly kiss on the cheek, saying something in his ear as she did so. Herr Kurtz nodded as he looked at the three Americans watching the greeting. She picked up the loaded basket and walked into the kitchen as Herr Kurtz walked over to the occupied table and asked the pilots if they would like another beer. Citing fullness caused by the dinner, all three declined.

Ingrid came out of the kitchen and glanced over at the table again. Reynolds, having been coming there the longest of the three, waved to her. Ingrid just stopped and glared, then ignored the wave and went up the stairs to the family apartment. The sound of the apartment door closing was more the sound of a drawbridge being raised against the oncoming enemy.

The three American pilots just looked at each other and shrugged their shoulders.

Chapter Three

The jeep was waiting for Matthews the next morning when he walked out the door of Frau Schlegal's house, its exhaust bellowing out the tailpipe as the warm air from the engine mixed with the cold wind swooping down from the vineyards and across the road. Matthews felt the chill the minute he opened up the house door and pulled the fur collar of his flight jacket up around his cheeks to protect them as he walked the few steps to the waiting vehicle. He grabbed the metal handle, opened the canvas door with its plastic window and climbed inside the barren metal container. The driver, different from the one the evening before, nodded a good morning, shifted into first gear with a grind, and headed to Rhein-Main and the operations building.

Once inside the operations building, Matthews was introduced to his Commander and the Operations Officer. He explained to them what experience he had, where he had been stationed and what he felt he was lacking. Both men listened as he detailed his flight training, his experiences in different aircraft, and what he wanted to gain from this assignment. Satisfied that he would fit into the squadron, they assigned him to a plane and went about introducing him to the rest of the pilots.

The next couple of weeks seemed like a blur. He flew every day, sometimes all day, to places he had only heard about. Places like Munich, the capital of

Bavaria located in the southeast portion of Germany, not far from Austria and Switzerland and the site of the renowned Oktoberfest. It was in Munich that Hitler had started his takeover of the German government, leading a group of men out of the basement of the Hofbrauhaus only to be arrested by the police and imprisoned. His second attempt was far more successful and the world had suffered as a result.

Matthews flew to Berlin a few times and was taken aback by the amount of destruction the city had endured. Circling the city, he had an opportunity to observe firsthand, the reconstructive efforts underway. Up close, he could still see the rubble of Hitler's bunker in front of the Brandenburg Gate and across the street from the Russian Tomb of the Unknown Soldier, still being constructed. Piles of rubble had been consolidated in areas where stylish buildings and fancy restaurants once stood as the city went about its business trying to regroup from the devastation of a losing war. Berlin, once the leading cosmopolitan city on the continent, lay in rubble. It struggled to rise from the ashes.

He was assigned a new co-pilot and navigator. They had been flying in Europe for a while longer than he had, so he listened and took in everything they said about the different airports they visited. The co-pilot, Mike Robson, had been a crew chief during the war and had seen more action than most. His squadron had been responsible for the deployment of infiltrators to the rear of enemy lines. Usually flying alone, his plane would attempt to skirt known anti-aircraft positions and deposit their living cargo in predetermined areas where they could cause damage to radar sites, fuel dumps, and even a few bridges. Towing a glider, he could release the cargo several miles from the designated target and be headed back home before the infantry had landed. Several times, however, the glider was not the answer and Robson had been forced to fly closer to the target so that the parachutists would not have to walk too far to the target. It was these flights that raised the hair on the back of the neck. After the war, Robson had gone to transition school to become a pilot. So while he had more experience flying in the European theater, he was a junior in rank to Matthews.

Larry Smiley was the navigator and his name was a true indicator of his personality. Always smiling, he was the joker of the squadron, thinking of gags and gimmicks to keep the laughter flowing. He was a good navigator but better morale booster, always ready with a joke and a pat on the back. Smiley never had aspirations to become a pilot, desiring instead to work his magic with maps. He constantly had a running battle with himself to see if he could plot a faster time from Point A to Point B. Above his fold-down desk in the plane he kept a list of his flight times to and from those points and was always trying to beat them.

The three men got along well.

Most of the flights were cargo flights with an occasional passenger. On a couple of occasions, he would fly back to England to pick up something, usually aircraft parts where they were needed in a hurry. On those flights he had the opportunity to stay overnight and renew acquaintances with the locals near the airfield. He had taken out one of the local women while he was stationed there, but soon found that absence did not make the heart grow fonder, just lonelier. While being cordial, she had made it clear that a long-distance relationship was not what she had in mind. He could understand that and agreed. He made a mental note to send her some flowers so there were no hard feelings.

Depending on the availability of transportation when his day was done, he ate in the mess hall and waited for transportation to become available which usually caused him to get back to the village late. The mess hall was a large open building with a kitchen at one end and the tables and chairs taking up the remainder of the room. Separating the kitchen from the dining area was a stainless steel railing wide enough to accommodate the laminated compartmentalized wooden trays the diners used to carry their food. Starting at one end, the crews would gather utensils and napkins, then slowly slide their trays along the railing, gathering first the rolls and make-believe butter, then moving to the single entrée, which a cook in semi-clean whites scooped onto a plate along with the proverbial potatoes and some type of vegetables. Desserts, usually slices of cakes or pies, completed the journey. On rare occasions, real ice cream, made in America, would be available, but if you were not one of the early ones to make it through the line, the only thing you saw was a round, empty cardboard container with a well-licked spoon lying at the bottom.

If transportation was available after he landed and did the post-flight check and debriefing, he would take it back to his room in the tiny village of Oberstdorf. Frau Schlegel would normally be in the parlor either reading or knitting, an afghan across her knees to ward off the chill of the evening. After a time, between his learning some German and Frau Schlegel learning a little English, they were able to carry on small conversations. She looked forward to his arrival because sometimes he would bring magazines that had been sent from the States for the troops to read. She enjoyed the pictures and usually had questions the following day after reading them. In that fashion, she learned her English.

One such evening, after cleaning up and changing clothes, Matthews went to zum Rose for dinner. He was becoming a regular now, like Tom Reynolds and Jim Wistick had become. When he opened the door, Herr Kurtz looked up from the bar and smiled. He liked the new American and was happy to see him frequent the restaurant.

Matthews waved his hand in "hello" and hung his flight jacket on the wooden stand. As Herr Kurtz retreated to the kitchen, Matthews walked over to his usual table and sat down, grabbing the menu from the center of the table and glancing over the list of items available. He knew what most of them were, but still had trouble remembering everything. He glanced up as the door opened and a gust of cold air entered the restaurant.

Ingrid walked in and closed the door behind her. She looked over at the lone American seated in her father's restaurant but made no motion of recognition. Removing her coat and scarf and hanging them on the opposite side of the wooden stand from Matthews, she walked deliberately toward the kitchen.

"Güten Abend," said Matthews.

Ingrid stopped in her tracks and looked over at Matthews. Without saying a word, she slapped his offering away with one disdainful look and continued into the kitchen. Matthews shrugged his shoulders and stared back at the menu.

"With a cold shoulder like that," thought Matthews, "the beer should really be chilled."

Over the course of the next couple of weeks, Matthews continued to try and engage Ingrid in a conversation. It had become almost a nightly ritual when he ate at the zum Rose, that he offered the salutation when she arrived at the restaurant from her daily job. The next couple of times after the first attempt, the result was the same, a cold look, the quick turning away of the head, and the deliberate march into the kitchen to say hello to her father. Her mission complete, she left the kitchen and went right upstairs to do whatever it was that she did up there. Herr Kurtz said nothing about it as he served Matthews his food.

After a couple of weeks, Matthews noticed a change in Ingrid's response. She no longer even looked at him when he said hello, but there was a slight upturning of the lips as though trying to contain a smile, acknowledging the little game they had come to play. He mentioned this to her father, who just shrugged his shoulders and walked away.

One night Matthews asked Herr Kurtz about his daughter and why she was not more open to his desire to be friends. Herr Kurtz, in his broken English, explained that his daughter wanted nothing to do with anyone in the military, be it the German military or the American. And especially wanted nothing to do with a pilot in either army; he slowly pulled out a chair at Matthews' table and sat down wearily and began to tell the story.

He explained that he, his wife, and Ingrid were living in a small town near the German-French border during the early part of 1943. While the war was going on, the only part that they could actually see were the occasional dog-fights between the Luftwaffe and the Allied fighter planes. Over the course of several months it had become routine to see them on a daily basis, sometimes several times a day. Inevitably, one fighter or the other would gain the upper hand with the other slowly sinking toward the earth, the telltale smoke bellowing from its fuselage.

On one such occasion, Herr Kurtz explained, he and Ingrid were returning to the house they rented after shopping at the local bakery. They stopped to watch the aerial show above them, as they occasionally did when outside. Two planes, one wearing the swastika of their home country, the other sporting the star of the American military, were dueling in the skies above them. Neither pilot seemed to have the upper hand to get a clear shot. Twisting and turning in the blue sky, the pilots attempted to outguess their opponent's next maneuver to gain the advantage.

Suddenly the German pilot put his plane into a dive, hoping to distance himself from the American attacker. The American pilot, as though pulled along on a string by the German plane, quickly followed at a steeper angle and closed the distance between the two. Its guns blazing, the American fighter raked the German plane with its fiery bullets till smoke and flames became evident. It was clear that on this day, the American was the victor.

Herr Kurtz and his daughter watched the death dance of the doomed fighter. As it headed to its fiery grave, it suddenly yawed to the left and came toward them. They froze in their tracks, unsure of what to do or where to go. The plane came closer and closer and they could almost smell the burning oil from the engine. Herr Kurtz threw his arms over his daughter and pulled her to the ground alongside of him as the screaming metal roared over their heads.

Looking up with horror, they saw the plane headed right for the house they were renting. With a scream, they both realized what was going to happen. The plane, now a firebomb, hit the brick house half-way up its front. As it pushed its way through the wall, its fuel tanks spewed their contents throughout the house, causing the house to become a funeral pyre for Frau Kurtz. The two just starred in horror, unable to do anything about it, yet unwilling to accept it. Hours later, surrounded by friends, the two finally left the scene to try and put into perspective what had happened.

Herr Kurtz finished the story with a sigh of resignation. As he stood up and pushed the chair under the table, he said that Ingrid blamed the death of her mother on the military, any military. It does not make any difference if it is French, German, English, or American. As a result, she refuses to have any connection with anyone in uniform.

"I," he said pointing to his leg, "understand the fortunes of war. But a young girl who loses her mother in an accident like that, cannot accept it without hating. And her hatred has landed on military personnel, especially those who fly. You are both."

Herr Kurtz slowly turned and walked back to the kitchen. Matthews watched as the man seemed to age with every step. Matthews now understood Ingrid's reluctance to even acknowledge him. He wondered what it would take if the situations were reversed. His mind drew a blank as he raised the glass mug and slowly sipped the frigid beer.

Chapter Four

The wheels of the grounded C-47 slowed as they neared the marks on the tarmac. Its nose, pointing to the sky, housed the three crew members who, unlike the attitude of the plane, were happy to be home.

"It's been a long week," thought Matthews. "Hell, it's been a long six weeks."

The crew had been flying almost every day for the last six weeks, and while Matthews loved to fly, even he had to have a rest now and then. So when the Operations Officer told him the day before yesterday that he would have the rest of the weekend off, he was very happy.

The flight that Saturday morning had been a routine hop to Munich and back. It was booked as a mail run, but in reality, it was a shuttle to allow some of the other pilots a chance to spend the weekend there. Munich was one of the favorite spots for the Americans. Besides the many clubs and breweries located in the city, it was only a short hop to Garmisch and the German Alps. Being early April, the snow was still plentiful and the skiing great. Since none of that interested Matthews, he was only too happy to make the short flight and get back home by noon.

The ground crew secured the wheels with the wooden chucks as Matthews and Robson went through their post-flight shutdown. By the time they were done with that, Smiley had put away the maps, locked up the fold-down table, and was already opening the door and handing out the ladder. He looked toward the cockpit as though asking permission to disembark. Matthews gave him a thumb's up, and Smiley scurried down the ladder and sprinted for the Operations building.

"Most have a hot date," thought Matthews. He envisioned the rest of his own day; a hot shower followed by a well-deserved nap, followed by a leisurely dinner at zum Rose.

"Perhaps Tom and Jim will be there and we can swap lies," he chuckled, thinking about the good times they have together.

The post flight check done, the pilots left the cockpit and walked through the cargo compartment to the open door. Matthews exited first and waited at the foot of the ladder as Robson stepped out and closed the airplane door behind him. As they walked past the other planes toward the Operations building, Smiley came darting out.

"I already did the debriefing," he yelled to them excitedly. "We're free till Monday morning! Have a great weekend!" With that, he turned and started jogging toward the billets, leaving the pilots surprised but happy that they were also done.

"Have a good weekend, Ron," said Robson. "As for me, a cold brew at the club is in order," he said miming the drinking of a frosted mug of good German beer.

Matthews chuckled as he walked away toward the waiting jeep. He had arranged that morning to have it ready when they got back so he did not have to waste any of his precious free time. The driver was standing there waiting and started the engine when he saw the pilot head his way. Matthews threw his flight bag in the back and climbed into the passenger seat.

"Let's get the heck outta Dodge, Sonny," his New York twang barely disguised by the bad Texas accent.

"Yes Sir," said the smiling driver. He pulled away from the Operations building and headed toward the front gate.

The trip to the village was a quick one and in no time Matthews found himself standing under a warm stream of water, some GI soap in one hand and a washcloth in the other. The shower felt good and he stayed in it a little longer than usual, mindful of the need to conserve the warm water, but luxuriating in its soothing caress. Feeling a little guilty, he stepped out of the shower and turned off the water. He dried himself off and wrapped the towel around his waist. He opened the door slightly and peered down the hall. Seeing no one, he grabbed his dirty uniform and quickly walked down the hall to his room. His bed had been freshly made and some colorful flowers in a vase placed on his dresser. He smiled as he thought of how much of a hostess Frau Schlegal was.

"If only she was forty years younger," he thought with a smile. And with that thought, he collapsed on the bed and fell asleep.

Matthews' eyes opened to a completely dark room. The sun had long set and the stars had taken its place. He could hear some movement downstairs in the kitchen and figured it was Frau Schlegal just cleaning up after dinner. He got out of bed, switched on the lamp on the nightstand and stretched to loosen the tight muscles that were reluctant to function. As he got dressed, his stomach growled as if to say it was its turn to get sated.

He went downstairs and walked to the kitchen door. His knock startled Frau Schlegel and she quickly turned to see what or who it was.

"Essen, Essen," he said. "Zum Rose."

She nodded knowingly and Matthews turned and walked down the hallway to the front door.

The gasthaus was empty except for an elderly couple sipping a couple glasses of wine. Matthews went to his usual corner table and sat down. Herr Kurtz saw him, waved, and went behind the bar to get him a beer. Ingrid walked out of the kitchen, glanced his way, and continued toward the elderly couple with their check. She said something to them, smiled, and went back into the kitchen, this time not even glancing at Matthews.

"Danke," said Matthews as Herr Kurtz set the mug on the table. He knew exactly what he wanted so he ordered a salad, cordon bleu, and French fries without looking at the menu. Herr Kurtz nodded in acknowledgment and walked back to the kitchen, returning in a minute with the salad.

He was finishing up his salad and the elderly couple were putting on their coats, ready to leave, when two young men walked into the restaurant. They wore tight pants tucked into high black boots and brown shirts under their worn leather jackets, imitating what had been the traditional dress for the now disbanded Hitler Youth. Their hair, short on top and almost none on the sides was definitely military and their manner was more like the police than

41

someone looking to get something to eat. The leader appeared to be the taller of the two, his short blond hair almost invisible. The shorter one had dark hair and a scowl on his face that looked permanent.

Matthews looked at the two young men but thought nothing about it. Meanwhile, the elderly couple hurriedly put on their coats and walked to the door. As they passed the men, they lowered their eyes as if by not seeing the men, the men would not see them. The door slammed as the couple left, leaving Matthews alone in the room.

The two men looked around the room, the taller one saying something to the other, and finally chose a table close to where the elderly couple had been seated. Ingrid walked out of the kitchen and saw the two leather jackets at the table. She turned around and went back to the kitchen, followed by whistles and words that Matthews did not understand.

Herr Kurtz carried the cordon bleu as he walked from the kitchen and sat it down in front of Matthews, most of the time starring at the two visitors. Matthews looked questioningly at Herr Kurtz, as if to ask who the men were.

"Hitler Junge," said Herr Kurtz with contempt. "Schieze," the German word for shit.

Matthews had heard of the Hitler youth, but thought that they had been disbanded and outlawed. Apparently this was the case in larger cities, but in some of the smaller villages, the group or what was left of it, still existed. Judging from the reaction of the elderly couple, the movement in Oberstdorf was still a threat.

Herr Kurtz turned and walked back toward the kitchen, starring again at the two men. Stopping halfway there, he looks them straight in the eye and spits on the floor.

"Schieze," he says to them and spits again.

The two young men jumped out of the chairs and rushed toward Herr Kurtz. The elderly German turned and faced his attackers like he was 30 years younger, but he was no match for them. The leader got to him first and shoved him in the chest with both hands. This caused the owner to lose his balance and stumbled backward with a yell. The small man saw the wooden leg and lashed out with his boot to strike it just below the knee. With a groan, the struggling owner was shoved back against the bar and the two men started beating him with their leather clad fists. He struggled to protect his face with his arms but he was not being successful.

Matthews quickly got up out of his chair and rushed the two men. The element of surprise allowed him to almost tackle the smaller of the two attackers and push him into one of the tables on the other side of the room. Out of the corner of his eye, Matthews saw Ingrid emerge at the kitchen door and quickly run to the other end of the kitchen. The taller attacker had stopped the barrage of blows on Herr Kurtz and was taking aim on Matthews, the gloved fist shot toward his head, but a quick parry with a forearm prevented it from landing. A second blow landed harmlessly on his shoulder.

Matthews stepped forward and jabbed with his left hand, hitting the offender on the right cheek and staggering him a little. A second jab caught him a little more squarely and sent him backward. Matthews cocked his right arm to finish the job, but before he could unleash his fist, powerful arms grabbed his arms and pulled them behind his back.

Realizing this must be the smaller thug, Matthews shoved backward with his body hoping to push the assailant into a wall, knocking his breath out and freeing himself from the iron grip. Crashing backward through the tables and chairs, he had almost reached his objective when a gloved fist crashed into his stomach, causing him to bend over in pain while he tried to regain his own breath. A second blow caught him on the left side of his face. He could hear the crunch of cartilage as his nose reacted to the punishment. His left ear was ringing.

The leader said something in German which Matthews did not understand, but when it was followed with another blow to the face, he decided it was not a pleasantry. A second blow to the stomach doubled him over and a punch to the back of the head dropped him to the floor. His face was bleeding now and he was coughing blood, doubled over to protect himself from the black boots kicking at his groin and face.

The rain of punishment stopped as the ringing in his ears turned to sirens. The two attackers stood still for a minute, then turned and rushed through the kitchen and out the back door. Seconds later, the half dozen police crashed through the front door and surveyed the situation.

Matthews was laying on the floor curled up into a ball. Blood was all over his face from his broken nose and he was moaning and clutching his stomach. Herr

Kurtz was leaning against the bar, trying to catch his breath, not able to say anything. Ingrid came running into the room, right to her father, and helped him to one of the few chairs not broken. As she turned to the police, she saw them pulling Matthews to his feet and trying to put handcuffs on him.

"Nein," Ingrid yelled angrily as she left her father's side and rushed to Matthews.

Quickly she explained to the police what had happened, describing the two attackers and telling them that the thugs had escaped out the back door. Two of the policemen quickly ran into the kitchen and out the back. A third one ran out to the cars to radio in the situation. While Ingrid continued to talk to the head policeman, the remaining two helped Matthews to a chair.

One of the policemen who had ran out the back door came back in a rush. He said something to the head policeman who in turn said something to the two remaining cops. He turned and headed to the door followed by one who had helped Matthews. The other policeman watched as they left, apparently remaining in case the attackers came back.

Herr Kurtz was breathing regularly now and was able to stand. Matthews was still hurting and Ingrid went into the kitchen to get a wet cloth. The older German walked over to Matthews and stuck out his hand.

"Danke," he said wearily. "Danke."

The coldness of the cloth felt good against his torn skin as Ingrid gingerly wiped the blood off his face.

"Yes, thank you very much," she said in perfect English.

Chapter Five

Two tiny elves with wooden sledgehammers were taking turns hitting a huge tree stump inside of Matthews' brain. He pulled the covers up over his head, hoping that the darkness would cause them to stop their incessant pounding, but all it seemed to do was to increase their vigor as the pounding grew harder and harder. His eyes opened.

"Herr Matthews," said Frau Schlegel in her frail voice as she knocked on the door. "Bitte kommen. MP's, Herr Matthews, MP's."

"I'll be right there, Frau Schlegel," he said as he struggled to get out of bed.

He slowly swung his legs over the side of the bed, his body resisting every movement which dragged it away from the horizontal position in which it so desperately wanted to remain. Being unsuccessful, it retaliated by achingly reminding Matthews of the beating he had put it through the night before. Sore all over, Matthews nevertheless managed to get semi-dressed and, slowly walking to the door and past the mirror, glancing at a visible reminder of the evening's activities. The left side of his face was black and blue, with his left eye swollen and almost shut. His nose seemed to have taken a right turn and was pointing 30 degrees to starboard. If it had not been so painful, it would have been comical.

Matthews stepped down off the last step and turned into the living room. Two military police had been sitting and now stood up at his approach.

"Sir," said the ranking Sergeant, "there was a report of you being in some kind of a fight. Guess the report was correct. The CO told us to check on you and bring you back to talk with him about the situation."

"Understand," nodded Matthews. "How did he find out?"

"Guess the Polizei filed a report this morning, first thing. It appears you may be some kind of a hero or something, Sir."

Matthews glanced down at his wrist where normally his watch would have been.

"What time is it, Sergeant?"

"Almost noon, Sir."

"Give me a couple of minutes to get properly dressed and I'll be right down," said Matthews as he turned to go up the stairs.

"Yes Sir, we'll wait right here."

The ride to the base seemed longer than usual as the bumps and ruts in the road deliberately jumped in their path. Compared to the ride, the meeting with the CO was relatively short. He had received the report from the Polizei about the fight the night before. Based on the statements by Herr Kurtz and his daughter, Matthews had been exonerated of any wrong, and in fact, had been portrayed in the report as the one who had protected both of them. The CO, interested in the well being of his men, wanted to see Matthews first hand and make sure he was all right. Seeing he was alive and was going to be all right, but

47

needing some medical attention, Matthews was ordered to the Flight Surgeon for an examination and whatever treatment the doctor deemed necessary.

The Flight Surgeon gave Matthews a thorough going-over, cleaning up the cuts on his face and even repositioning the nose, though that was painful. A quick snap and it was back in place and a piece of tape across the bridge of the nose attempted to hold it in place; the tape was more of a reminder, as the nose would stay in place unless, of course, it came across a gloved hand again. Matthews hoped that would not happen.

Before leaving the Flight Surgeon's office, Matthews was informed that he would be off flight status for a week until his eye swelling went away. Though he protested, the doctor refused to change his order and Matthews left the office carrying a "no flight status" notice to the Operations building and some pain medicine. Before that notice could be canceled, he would have to make another appointment with the doctor to get his blessing. The military was strict about that.

The MP jeep was waiting at the Operations shack to take him back to Oberstdorf. They dropped him at the front door, saluted, and headed back toward the airfield. He walked in the front door and saw Frau Schlegel sitting in the living room.

"Alles Gut?" she questioned.

"Ja," replied Matthews heading up the stairs, "Alles Gut."

His bedroom door was slightly ajar and entering he found that the bed had been made, the window cracked to let in some fresh air. With the pain

48

medicine beginning to take hold, he laid back down on the bed he had so reluctantly left a couple of hours earlier and fell asleep.

The body, whether due to the return to the horizontal position or to the pain medicine, let the tired pilot sleep. Even the elves quit banging on the stump.

Chapter Six

By the time that Matthews' body allowed him to tortuously stand up again, the whole day had gone by. The sun had run its course and the moon shone brightly down from the star-filled sky. "That is a good thing," Matthews thought, "because squinting in the strong sun would just cause his face to ache." The medicine the doc had given him had done its job, causing the body to rest so as to self-heal. While the remnants of the fight could still be seen on his face, his body reacted less strenuously when he asked it to resume the vertical position. A quick jerk and the tape across his nose was gone, replaced with a slight bump which would probably never go away.

Matthews, clad in his olive drab army-issued boxers, grabbed a soft towel that Frau Schlegal had left in his room and slowly made his way down the hall to the shower. The hot water eased more of the pain, as the muscles reacted to the soothing touch of the warmth. Carefully, Matthews allowed the stream of water to wash over his face, mindful of the need for caution in seeing how his injured nose would react. The damaged cartilage twitched when the heat touched it, then seemed to slip into a state of euphoria, relishing both the massage of the stream of water and the heat it brought along with it. Matthews closed his eyes and allowed his body to absorb all there was to absorb.

The exterior of the body now sated, Matthews quickly changed into civilian clothes, gingerly walked down the stairs, smiled briefly at Frau Schlegal, and made his way to zum Rose. Spotted by Herr Kurtz as he entered, Matthews found himself the center of attention of all diners in the restaurant with hands reaching out to shake his and pat him on the shoulders. Herr Kurtz escorted him to his standard table, shouted something over his shoulder to the kitchen, and made sure that he was comfortable.

Looking up from the table, Matthews saw Ingrid walking toward him, her right hand carrying a cold mug of local beer, and her left hand holding a vase of flowers. She approached him and placed the flowers in the middle of the table, the cold mug in front of him. A smile, not well hidden, adorned her face.

"Thank you again, Lieutenant, for your help last night. You have proven yourself a friend of my father's, and thus mine. Tonight, dinner will be our pleasure. Please order whatever you wish."

"Thank you, Ingrid, it is Ingrid isn't it? We have never been formally introduced," he said.

"Yes, it is Ingrid and I will be serving you this evening. I hope that is not a problem."

"Problem?" he questioned. "It would be a pleasure."

She smiled, not hiding it at all this time, turned slowly and walked directly back to the kitchen, ignoring the stares of the other astonished customers.

The rest of the evening was a blur to Matthews. Mindful of Herr Kurtz's tough economic situation, he chose his usual items. But it didn't seem to matter what he ordered, Ingrid delivered the best of everything the house had to offer. If he ordered veal, she would bring him the veal dish, but also the best beef they had in house. When he ordered a house salad, she served him the house salad, mixed with the vegetables either just coming into season, or those just going out. And the three kinds of potatoes she brought to the table was more than a dozen men could eat. The only thing she brought him that he ordered was the cold beer. It was never more than half empty when a new cold mug would magically appear, the old one taken away to go where half empty mugs go.

When the stomach yelled "Stop!" Matthews pushed back from the table, released a sigh of contentment, or relief depending on your perspective, and slouched in the chair like a man who was one forkful away from exploding. Lifting his head, he saw both Herr Kurtz and Ingrid standing in front of him. Herr Kurtz extended his hand and the two men clasped hands like knowing brothers.

Ingrid stuck out her hand and Matthews gently took it in his. She gave the clasp a short shake, then just stood there, holding his hand. Her mouth said "Thank you," but her eyes said something else. Matthews thought about it the whole walk home.

The rest of the week slid by quickly. Not seeing the Flight Surgeon for a week gave Matthews time to see more of the area. But since there were no vehicles, he did a lot of walking. For the first time since arriving to Obertsdorf, he crossed the street from Frau Schlegal's and walked up the slope of the vineyard, between the rows of grapes, to the ruins of the tower he had previously spotted.

The tower itself was not in very good shape, having witnessed hundreds of years of environmental assaults, not to mention the assaults of armies desiring to claim the area as their own. Struggling a little to reach the top, he saw that he had been right about look-out post. This was not a large castle, home to royalty and protector of villages alike. No, this was an isolated outpost, probably manned by the dregs of the army at that time, and considered Siberia to the Germanic tribes who manned it.

He found a patch of grass near the tower and sat down, viewing the town from a new perspective. He could see the whole thing, one main road through the center of town, four, no, five streets off the main road, each ending at what looked to be a large farm growing primarily grapes for the local wine. It was clear that the village started as a farming village and only when other occupations began to spring up, were the single homes along the ancillary streets without the farmland built.

He saw the building housing zum Rose and wondered about Ingrid. After the first night, she had continued to wait on tables, not always his, but always with a glance in his direction. She would stop by and say hello, always with a smile, and their light banter back and forth had aroused much interest among the locals, most of whom called her the "iron-hearted girl."

Herr Kurtz had seen a change in his daughter and pointed it out to Matthews, with a knowing smile on his face. Matthews had begun looking forward to visiting the zum Rose. His walking during the day had kept his mind off his lack of flying, and seeing

Ingrid in the evening was a highlight of the day. He had learned that she had attended a French Catholic school growing up when they were living near the France border. She had a propensity for languages, learning English and French fluently, and enough Spanish to get by. She was attending school during the day, hoping to become a teacher upon completion, and working with her father at the restaurant when not studying in the evening. Slowly, he was beginning to learn about her, and her him. Her questions concerning the United States reflected book knowledge of the country, but lacked the insight into everyday living which reflected the realities of the United States. Only by living there could somebody learn the country. But then, that is true for all countries.

"Today is Friday," Matthews thought to himself. "On Monday I have to report back to the Flight Surgeon. Hopefully the week's rest will have done its trick and I can resume flying. Wonder what missions the guys have flown since I was grounded? Oh well, we'll find out on Monday."

Matthews could tell by the sun's angle in the western sky that the early evening was not far away. He carefully made his way through the vines, down the hill, and back to his room, noticing that Frau Schlagel was busy in the kitchen preparing something. He took an unusual second shower of the day, a quick one, and got dressed. She was still in the kitchen as he slipped out the door and headed to the zum Rose.

Both Tom Reynolds and Jim Wistick were seated at a table and seeing Matthews, they waved him over.

He looked around the restaurant for Ingrid, but saw only some other diners, some of whom waved to him and smiled. He sat down with the two pilots and questioned them on the week's activities. They had both been very busy, flying two, sometimes three missions a day. They were looking forward to the weekend and being able to sleep in a couple of days.

Herr Kurtz brought over Matthews' beer and sat it down in front of him. Ingrid came out of the kitchen and looked over at Matthews, hesitantly starting to wave to him, but seeing the other two Americans, went about her business with the other customers. Within fifteen minutes, the two pilots finished their dinner and headed back to their respective rooms, leaving Matthews alone to finish his dinner which was fine with him, for he sensed that Ingrid did not want to show him any attention with the other Americans around.

His sense was correct, for as soon as the others had left, Ingrid came over to his table to say hello. She smiled and held out her hand. He took it gently and said something about how smooth it was. Her smile grew bigger, and even bigger yet as she reported that she had done real well on her last test of the semester and could start to think about the summer months and a little relaxation.

"Well congratulations, that is wonderful," he said. "We have to celebrate!"

Ingrid looked at him a little strangely.

"Look, when somebody accomplishes something in our country, we like to celebrate with them and give them a special feeling of accomplishment. It is our way of sharing in achievement. I am sure that you

55

have something of a similar tradition, right? You don't have any school tomorrow do you?"

"No," said Ingrid. "It's all over for the summer."

"OK, that settles it then. We will do something together to celebrate your achievement. But, quite honestly, I am a little at a loss to think of something to do. Do you have any suggestions?"

Ingrid thought for a moment. "Bad Durkhiem," she said.

"Bad Durkhiem?

"A wine fest, a celebration of wine in this small village not far from here. It is known the country over and is a lot of fun with wine, games, music, and food. It lasts for two weeks, but this is the first weekend. It won't be as crowded this weekend as next. It will be fun.

Matthews was thinking about the need for a jeep or some other means of transportation. He didn't want to take the bus, as then you were tied to the bus schedule. Ingrid somehow knew what he was thinking.

"We don't use it much, but my father has a car in the garage behind the restaurant and I have a license. We can take that. I'll pick you up at noon and we'll have something to eat before leaving; that way we'll have something in our stomachs when we get there. I'll tell my father we will be back late so he won't worry and we will celebrate, American-style," she said with a smile on her face.

"Deal," he said, and reached out to shake her hand and cement the plan.

She slipped her hand in his and they looked at each other for what seemed like decades. Slowly, he raised her hand to his lips and lightly placed a kiss on the back of her hand. She stared at him for an eternity, slowly withdrew her hand from his and kissed her hand at the exact spot he had kissed her. Their eyes were glued to each other, and as she turned to walk away, a quick glance over her shoulder told him that there was more to come.

That evening couldn't pass quickly enough and Matthews tossed and turned all night. He wondered what the morning would bring, what if he was getting over his head, what if his wanting a relationship with this girl was just the result of being far from home. He wondered a lot of things. Finally, at three in the morning, the wondering stopped and fatigue started, putting him to sleep for a few hours till the morning sun brought a new day.

Chapter Seven

The small faded blue Volkswagen slowly pulled in front of Frau Schlegel's dark house and rolled to a stop. The wooden shutters were still pulled down even though it was close to 10:30 in the morning and the day was almost half way done. Ingrid sat in the car and waited.

Ron heard the car pull up to the house and stop, its engine winding down and finally quitting. He didn't bother looking out the window to see if it was Ingrid. He knew the sound of a military jeep and it decidedly was not one of those. Since no one else was expected, he guessed it was Ingrid and quickly finished getting dressed. He was looking forward to this day and didn't want to miss a minute of it. Glancing at the mirror, he thought "B+," smiled and left his room, quietly closing the door behind him in case Frau Schlegel was taking a nap. He floated down the stairs and out the front door.

"Güten Morgan," he said in the best German accent he could muster.

"Güten Morgan," she replied smiling. "How are you?" quickly switching to English.

"Doing great, thanks! I am looking forward to having a wonderful day and celebrating your graduation. And this will be the first time that I will be out and among your people so it will give me a chance to learn more about your country – and you."

She glanced over at him and smiled, slipped the car into first gear, and slowly pulled away, heading for what she hoped was a very nice and pleasant day.

The drive to Bad Durkheim was only about 30 minutes but during that time he learned much about his guest country. For example, she had explained to him that the word "Bad," such as in Bad Durkheim, meant "bath" and had been used by the Romans during their occupation to designate cities where there were hot baths to soothe the tired muscles. Cities such as Bad Durkheim, Bad Kreuznach, and Bad Muenster were all known for their hot mineral springs which flowed freely from the ground. Baden, the site of well-used mineral baths by Roman legions, had in fact grown up to become a world-renowned resort town, boasting one of the classiest casinos in Europe. It was a place that wealthy Germans would visit to relax, enjoy the springs, dine well, and take their chances at the roulette wheel.

The drive through German countryside was very interesting. Besides listening to Ingrid speaking about her beloved country, Ron was able to view the small towns and their vineyards on an up-close and personal basis rather than from thousands of feet above. Instead of viewing the houses through a small window at a speed of 120 miles per hour, he was able to see them brick by brick, layer upon layer, window by window. He saw the curtains hanging inside the windows, the small mailboxes hanging near the front door, and the small, square metal boxes on the stoop which housed empty milk bottles until they were replaced with full ones every other day.

He also saw women walking to and from the Lebensmittle, the local grocery store they visited daily to purchase the food to be consumed that day. Baskets hanging from their arms carried the daily finds of sausage, vegetables, potatoes, and perhaps a container of homemade soup. Sometimes these women were accompanied by their little daughters, too young to attend school, but old enough to follow their mothers on their daily routine. Dutifully carrying their own little baskets, these young girls learned early on the methods for selecting the just-ripe fruits and vegetables needed to nourish their future families. The world was on the mend and it was being done village by village.

The sign said "Bad Durkheim" as the Volkswagen slowed to allow several families to cross the street, heading toward the carnival area after parking their car. Ingrid inched her car ahead, looking for a parking space. A large field on the right opened up past a row of houses and they both could see the huge tents of the wine fest beyond the field. Cars filled the open spaces, but a small area near a tree seemed large enough to handle the Volkswagen. Ingrid made a right turn and deftly pulled into the spot. The leaves of the tree barely touched the roof as though caressing a new found friend or petting a new puppy. They opened their doors and stepped into the noisy air, looking at each other in anticipation of the fun to come.

It was a little after eleven in the morning, but it was Saturday and the fest was well on its way. Entering through a gate in a temporary fence that acted more as a boundary than as an impediment, the couple melted into the excited crowd. Much to Ron's surprise, many of the tents featured products of the local region displaying fruits and vegetables. Some tents contained handmade furniture, some blankets and quilts, while some others showed off new items designed to make life easier. It seemed to him that this was more of a state fair than a wine fest. But he spoke too soon.

Exiting one of the display tents he heard the music blaring from a large multi-colored tent on the other side of a large dirt walkway. Crowds of people walking in both directions formed a mobile human fence preventing them from getting to the music and the obvious good times surrounding the ompaa band. He hesitated a little, wanting to wade through the walkers, but not wanting to cause a scene.

Ingrid sensed his dilemma, so she grabbed his hand and started crossing against the crowd, yelling something in her native tongue as she pushed her way through, Ron gingerly in tow. The crowds seemed to part like the Red Sea and with very few bumps and bruises, they quickly found themselves on the other side of the walkway. He stood and looked back at the path they had just covered and wondered how they had gotten through the masses so quickly. He then remembered her yelling something as they moved.

"What were you yelling as we moved through the crowd?" he asked with a quizzical look on his face.

Ingrid smiled and laughed a little. "I told them you were a little crazy and needed a beer before you went berserk."

He looked at her smiling face not knowing if he should believe her or not and the more he looked, the bigger her smile became. He started to chuckle and as he did, she started to laugh and pretty soon they were both laughing at the silly trick they had pulled over the crowds.

"Come on," he said still chuckling, "let's go have a beer before I do go crazy!" he held his hand out and she looked at it before placing hers in his. They looked into each other's eyes, the smiles still there, and walked into the beer tent.

The beer tent covered an area about as large as a football field. Lining the two long sides of the structure were food and beer stations bustling with activity. Large grills, their exhaust hoods venting through the side of the tent, provided the heat to cook the usual bratwursts and bockwursts while several more grill stations were the set up to cook whole chickens, wild game, and some other things with which Ron was unfamiliar. Five or six people worked each grill station, eagerly providing the buxomly waitresses with their requested orders. Speed was of the essence, as the sooner the food was delivered, the sooner the patrons paid and the tips collected.

Interspersed between the grills were the beer stations. Ron noticed that there seemed to be twice as many beer stations as grills and the waitresses were two or three deep at each station. Men dressed in lederhosen, leather shorts held up with decorated suspenders, scrambled behind the stations filling large glass mugs with beer from portable taps, allowing the foam to spill over the top to ensure a complete fill. As a result, the dirt floor of the beer booths was wet and slippery, requiring the placement of wood panels to reduce the chances of sliding and spilling the precious cargo.

Visitors to this beer tent sat on long wooden picnic tables seating about ten people on a side depending on the size of the people. Ron guessed that there had to be close to 100 or more of these tables throughout the tent. Groups of people looking for seats settled for whatever was available and joined those already at the table. Despite not knowing each other, the conversations among the strangers became more and more boisterous as more and more empty mugs lined the center of the wooden tables.

The centerpiece of the structure was a large wooden platform in the middle of the tent from which the traditional German music emanated. The platform was raised about 8 to 10 feet off the floor, a wooden railing circling all but the area where the steps allowed the band to enter and exit the platform. Four sturdy poles supported a roof over the platform which was covered with thatched grass like a traditional Bavarian farm roof. The band members played their instruments with gusto, trying to ensure the far corners of its territory were duly entertained.

The band members themselves were wonders to behold. They all dressed in lederhosen, leather shorts with suspenders attached, a mostly-white shirt with various amounts of ruffles, and knee-high socks held up by garters. Heavy dark shoes completed the outfits and provided the support they needed to play for hours at a time. Instruments ranging from the traditional accordion and drums to the loud and brassy horns and trumpets brought the visitors to their feet and started the crowd swaying to the melodies of traditional songs. As Ron looked around the tent, he realized that while it was only noon, many people had been there for hours already and would soon be leaving to enjoy a much needed afternoon nap.

While Ron had been busy soaking up the atmosphere of his first wine fest, Ingrid had been busy looking for a place to sit. She pulled on Ron's hand and motioned to a half-full picnic table near the center of the tent, but far enough away from the music so as to allow for talking. Ron nodded and they made their way around and through the hustling waitresses to the waiting table. Ingrid slid onto the wooden bench first, nodding hello to the couple across the way. Ron followed, doing the same and offering his hand to the man. The man hesitated, then slowly raised his hand to Ron's, briskly shaking it upon contact. The rousing end to a brisk polka broke the moment as everyone at the table applauded the efforts of the popular band. Ron sat down and turned to Ingrid.

"Now let's get you that beer before you really go crazy," she said, motioning to one of the larger waitresses to come over. The haggard-looking woman completed her deliveries and moved over to their table.

"Bitte, ein grosses bier und eine weiss wein," said Ingrid. She turned to Ron and asked him if he was hungry. After his affirmative, she continued to the waitress, "Und zwei bratwurst mit Brot and Snef."

"I understood most of what you said, but what is Snef?" asked Ron.

"Snef is mustard, hot mustard, and adds just the right touch of spice."

"If you say so," smiled Ron as the band started a loud refrain to the delight of the roaring crowd.

"This is one of our favorite drinking songs and always gets the crowd going," explained Ingrid. "It starts out slow and gets faster and faster with each chorus and the crowd accompanies the band by banging on the tables, getting louder as they get faster. Watch."

Sure enough the crowd, including the couple sitting across the table, was starting to lightly tap on the wooden table, doubling now as a drum. As each chorus ended, a loud roar went up from the crowd and the music got faster and the banging got louder. He watched as Ingrid joined into the festivities.

After about the fourth chorus the man across the table caught Ron's eyes and, smiling, motioned him to join the banging. Ron nodded in return and began to do his part to fit in. Ingrid felt the vibrations of the table and turned to see what caused the sudden movement. She smiled when she saw Ron doing his best to fit in with the other people at the table and to enjoy himself. She turned back to the bandstand with a smile on her face.

The song ended with the crashing sound of hundreds of fists hitting the wooden tables at the same time, with smiles and raucous laughter filling the tent from end to end. Applause followed the band as it exited the bandstand for a well-deserved rest. Ron and Ingrid both took deep breaths and slumped over the table.

Magically, the largest beer mug that Ron ever saw appeared before him while a medium sized glass of white wine showed up in front of Ingrid. Immediately behind the drinks came the two bratwursts and two small rolls with a dab of yellow mustard on the plate beside each one. Ron went to reach into his pocket to pay, but Ingrid put her hand on his arm to stop him. The waitress reached across between them, and using white chalk, scribbled something on the table, turned and left. Ron looked puzzled as he looked at Ingrid.

"This is the way they keep track of how much you owe. Each type of line indicates what you have been served. For example, that straight line is a beer, the squiggly line is a wine, and those two oval circles are the bratwursts. A second beer would result in a second line, and so forth. It is a simple system and frees up more time for the waitresses to serve instead of making change after each delivery. Of course, honesty is essential in these situations, but there rarely seems to be a problem."

Ron listened and nodded his understanding as he reached for the mug. Little foam covered the top and he could see the clear golden liquid easily through the mug's glass. Ingrid grabbed her wine glass, raising it to lightly tap the much larger mug, and slowly sipped her drink. Ron followed suit, tasting the first cold beer of the day and savoring its typical German bitterness. A second sip immediately followed the first, a third following the second, and by the time the mug was replaced on the table, half of it was empty.

Ron looked embarrassed as he realized how much beer he had consumed in a matter of seconds. He vowed to keep a watch on his consumption, not wanting to ruin what, from all initial appearances, was going to be a very nice day with Ingrid. She looked at him, then at the mug, then back at him, smiled, and took another sip of her wine as if to say, "That's ok, I have my wine." The moment was interrupted by the shriek of the microphone as the master of ceremonies introduced the next band to play. The crowd laughed as the drummer punctuated the introduction with crashing cymbals and whacks on the snare drum, all the time laughing and urging the crowd on. The master of ceremonies finally gave up, and in a good natured gesture, threw up his hands and skipped to the stairs, waving as he slowly disappeared from sight.

The band burst into song and the crowd roared with approval.

The afternoon seemed to slip away. Ingrid took Ron around the whole fest area, stopping at several more beer tents along the way. At each one, they had the now traditional beer and wine, sometimes with additional food, sometimes without. And as they moved from place to place, their attraction to each other seemed to grow.

Ingrid liked the quiet swagger of the American pilot, his confidence masked from most by his unfamiliarity with the German culture he was experiencing for the first time. But she watched his eyes as they took in the events of the afternoon and realized that he was constantly watching and learning from the little things around him. But more than learning what to do, he was assimilating the reasons behind the doing, mentally filing away important pieces of German thinking while quickly discarding those which were lager-inspired. She liked that about him. He was not the typical solder, German, American or otherwise. He was performing his duty as a soldier, but he was not a soldier. He was more than that and she wondered what the future had in store for him.

It was about 7:30 in the evening when the two of them sunk down on a bench alongside the main walkway of the wine fest. They had been at it the better part of the day, and both sensed that the other one was tired and wanted to rest. But neither of them wanted the day to end. What had started out as a cordial relationship had begun to blossom into something more. The initial hand-holding was replaced with arms around each other's' waist, little messages whispered into ears, and the slight brush of one set of lips against another, something that happened without any planning or forethought. It was just the right thing to do at the time. Drawing back from that initial kiss, they looked into each other's eyes and both knew they wanted more.

"Do you think we should be getting back?" Ron asked as he held Ingrid's hand, his words saying one thing, his voice saying another.

Ingrid heard the real question in his voice. "Yes," she said, "before the wine takes over completely."

Not saying anything else, they got up from the bench and started walking back to the car, struggling against both the crowds that were coming for the evening activities and the effects of the alcohol they had consumed. It took a minute to find the car, but there it was, still under the tree, the leaves of the branches resting easily across the roof. Ron guided her around to the driver's door and after she unlocked it, held it open for her until she was seated inside. He then walked around to the other side, pleasantly surprised that she had opened his door, and plopped himself in the passenger seat.

The ride back to the village took a little more time than the ride to the fest. Ingrid was very careful with her driving, making sure that the effects of the wine did not overcome her judgment while driving. Ron sat alongside her, his eyes an extension of hers, constantly on the lookout for any potential conflicts. Forty-five minutes after leaving the parking lot, Ingrid pulled up in front of Frau Schlegel's house and stopped.

Ron looked at her as the car stopped. "Would you like to come up to my room?" he asked, holding his breath waiting for her answer.

She looked through his eyes and into his heart, reading the affection that had grown during the day. She wondered about the timing of his request, and of her response. How much was real and how much was the alcohol? Would she be better off waiting or was now the time? Her mind raced back to her utter dislike for anything in uniform, but her heart saw him without a uniform; without the prejudices that went with it. He was a man, not a symbol, and she saw him as such.

"Yes," she said.

They walked up the stairs together, holding onto the railing to keep themselves steady. In opening the front door he had dropped his key and Ingrid had picked it up and put it into her pocket. They reached the top of the stairs and he pointed to the door to his room, his little sanctuary from the outside world. He opened the door and ushered her in, leaning against it to keep from stumbling. He closed the door behind them and she turned and looked at him. He walked toward her and held his arms open.

She moved toward him and his arms encircled her, his lips searching for hers. She tilted her head upwards, and they kissed. He led her to the bed, still kissing, and laid down on the bed, pulling her on top of him. She fit neatly into the folds of his body and he could feel her warmth spreading to both of them. His hands began to caress her body and he sensed her pleasure by the little moans that escaped from her throat and the movements of her body as she sought to get closer to him.

"So this is what it's like to be loved," thought Ron as he began to unbutton the back of her dress.

Suddenly Ingrid stopped. She lifted her head and looked him straight in the eye. Her moment of hesitation was too much for Ron. He froze, a puzzled look on his face.

"No," said Ingrid. "This is not how I want it to happen. I don't want it to be influenced by the amount of wine or beer we had. I don't want to wonder later on if it was love or lust that drove us together. I want to know it is the real thing. I want it to be the result of our love for each other. And I need to know in my heart that this is something I want, not for just the moment, but forever."

She rolled off of him and stood up; swaying a little as she straightened her dress to make sure everything was where it should be in case she met Frau Schlegel on the way out

"Ron," she said, "this has been one of the nicest days of my life. Thank you for making me realize that I can be happy with someone. That my life is not

70

destined to go through this world alone. That I can, that it is possible despite my ingrained reluctance, to care for somebody. That," and she hesitated, "I can love someone."

Ingrid turned and walked to the door. Reaching it, she turned to Ron and blew him a kiss.

"Good night, love," she said with one of the sweetest voices he had ever heard.

The door closed behind her

He turned over and passed out.

Chapter Eight

Ron rolled over, reaching for the covers to ward off the chill of the night. His hand groped for the quilt but found nothing. Irritated, he opened his eyes and found himself staring up at the ceiling.

"What is going on?" he thought.

Slowly he turned his head to the right and his eyes focused on the dresser against the wall. He shifted his view to the left and the top of the bed gradually came into focus. He realized that he was lying cross-wise on the bed and, after further investigation, was still in the same clothes he had worn when he and Ingrid went to the wine fest.

"Oh no," he thought, "what did I mess up last night!" His memory went back to the end of the day and he remembered kissing Ingrid and pulling her down on top of him. He then vaguely remembered her getting up and saying something, then leaving. The rest of his memory failed him.

He looked at his watch and, barely able to focus, saw that it was sometime between 3 and 3:30 in the morning. He slowly got up and took off his shoes and shirt, leaving on his pants so he could carefully walk to the bathroom at the end of the hall. His mouth tasted like stale beer and he grabbed his toothbrush and toothpaste to take with him. He cautiously negotiated the hall to the bathroom, did what had to be done and slowly made his way back to his room.

Pulling back the covers, Ron gingerly sat on the edge of the bed and removed his pants. Like being sucked into a whirlwind, his body fell back onto the bed, his legs snaking under the covers which now protected him from the early morning chill. His head settled softly onto the pillows and he slowly fell into a deep sleep, made all the more pleasant by the thoughts of Ingrid.

Ron sensed more than heard the door slowly open. He didn't know if it was a dream or not and refused to open his eyes to find out. He was still tired from the night before and even going to bed early, actually more like passed out, had not satisfied his need for rest. In truth, the only rest he had had was after waking up around 3 and settling himself into a more proper sleeping position. He was not going to disturb that now.

Eyes closed, he replayed the events of the day before in his mind. He recalled the drive to the wine fest and the interesting discussion he and Ingrid had concerning the Roman baths. He recalled his first visit to a beer tent and the fun they had singing and carousing with the locals. He remembered a couple more of the tents, some more beer, and then a couple more tents.

But most of all, he remembered getting to know Ingrid and how they seemed to become closer and closer as the day wore on. Holding hands, dancing close, laughing, oh yes, lots of laughter, and the comfortable feeling of being with someone.

He remembered the ride home, her coming up to his room and into his arms. He remembered falling on to the bed and...then she left. He couldn't remember if she was mad or angry or hurt or what. Just that she left.

He felt the edge of the bed sag a little and a finger press softly against his lips. He opened his eyes and shook his head, trying to clear the cobwebs from his mind and focus on what was there.

Ingrid sat on the edge of the bed, smiling her beautiful smile, bundled up in a warm coat, protection against the same chill that had found him earlier. Her finger pressed against his lips to stop him from saying anything that would alert Frau Schlegel.

"Good morning, dear," she said in a soft whisper.

"Good morning," he replied, his voice not as steady as hers and with a bit of wonderment. "What are you doing here? And how did you get in?"

"Ah, the beer has taken its toll, and the memory is the first thing to go," she laughed quietly. "Don't you remember dropping your keys on the way upstairs last evening? I picked them up and put them in my purse so they didn't get lost. They came in handy this morning."

"But you left last night, before, before anything happened. Why did you do that?"

"You don't remember?" she asked.

Ron shook his head in reply. "No, I don't."

"You and I were on the bed and you started to unbutton my dress. I wanted us to make love more than anything else I have ever wanted. But I wanted it to be the product of a real desire, not the type brought on by too much beer or too much wine, or a combination of both. It had to be fueled by the feelings each one has for the other and the desire to please each other now, and be with each other for eternity. Love is not a short term trip, nor, in my mind, is it to be entered into without a true understanding of the effort required to keep it going. Continuing last night would have cast a pall over a beautiful thing because I would always wonder if it was real or contrived. Regardless of where the future would have taken us, that thought would have dogged me the rest of my days. That is not how love should start and definitely not how it should be...at least not for me."

"I am sorry," Ron said, "I didn't mean to offend you in any way at all. It just felt right, us being together I mean, and so comfortable. I even sensed that you wanted it too. Perhaps I was wrong."

"Ron Matthews, you are not wrong. The desire was, is there. The timing was wrong. Why do you think I came here this morning?"

He looked up into her eyes and they literally laughed at him, not a ridiculing laughter, but a laughter that was about to bring joy to someone else. He had seen that type of laughter before, and he recognized it as the look in his mother's eyes when she woke him up on Christmas morning to take him downstairs to the Christmas tree. It was a family tradition that no kids went downstairs until the parents went down first, and it was his mother who woke the kids up and shepherded them downstairs, that same look in her eyes.

Ingrid continued to smile as she stood up and slowly took off her coat, letting it drop to the floor. Ron couldn't believe his eyes. There stood Ingrid in a floor-length transparent, white negligee clinging ever so slightly to the roundness of her breast and hips.

The smallness of her waist made the roundness more pronounced and the low neckline drew the eyes toward her ample bosoms. She knew she had his attention and that pleased her.

Leaning forward, she playfully knocked on the mattress. "Can I come in?" she softly whispered.

Ron shifted over to the side of the bed and raised the covers for Ingrid to slip under. "Come into my parlor, said the spider to the fly," intoned Ron.

"With pleasure," said Ingrid as she slid under the covers, pulling them up to her neck and turning to face him.

"Now, where were we?" she moaned as her body pressed against his, feeling him grow at her touch. "Please don't be long," she pleaded as his lips began moving down to her stomach and his hands traced the outline of her body.

"Pleeeeeeeease!"

Chapter Nine

Ron and Ingrid continued to see each other every day, and while their intimate moments together were somewhat restricted because of their living situation, they enjoyed being in each other's company so much that when the opportunities arose, it was an added benefit. One of which they took full advantage.

Winter and spring had gone and the German summer was into June, 1948. Germany, under the western countries, began to reorganize itself from a conquered nation to a sovereign country. This move was fully supported by the United States, in fact was prompted by the United States. Instead of seeing Germany as a conquered nation, the U.S. was looking to use Germany, the sovereign country, as a buffer country between itself and what it perceived as an aggressive Soviet Union and other Soviet bloc countries.

However, the Soviet Union was not thrilled with the idea of a reconstituted Germany. Hitler's open violation of the peace pact made with Stalin and the way the Soviet people had been treated by the German army made the Soviet government extremely leery of any sort of reunited Germany. It had been a long and hard struggle to defeat the Germans. They had done it, but not without mistakes made by the German war planners and the luck of an ugly winter.

They had no desire to even remotely face the prospect again and the loss of so many people.

Ron and Ingrid talked about the new German government and its implications. Ingrid was a strong believer that all of Germany should be united as before. In her mind, there was no West Germany nor East Germany. There was Germany, and that is how it should be.

Ron, fully mindful of Ingrid's belief, was more of a realist. He understood that the Soviet Union would not allow the defeated country to reunite. It was not about to give up land for which its soldiers had died. Ingrid understood that also, but still wanted a single Germany.

They spent many evenings discussing the situation, listening to the political speeches on the radio from both sides. The war of words between the Soviet and Western sides continued to escalate and in one particular speech, Winston Churchill spoke of the "Iron Curtain" which ran symbolically down the middle of Europe and separated the East from the West. Unknown to both of them, this phrase was to define the separation for decades to come.

Meanwhile, they continued to learn more about each other and as they did, their affection for each other also grew. Nightly dinner became a ritual and occasional nights together became a luxury they both enjoyed. Ingrid's father had welcomed the American pilot into their family, especially as he saw the changes in Ingrid and how happy she had become with her life. What had once been a young girl mired in solace and pity now stood a confident woman looking forward to the next day and the joy it would bring. Occasionally they were able to get away for a weekend, depending on Ron's flight schedule, and they enjoyed that time to the fullest. The creation of the German state continued to make progress. A Central Bank was established to combat the black market caused by the overabundance of currency and the scarcity of goods and to aid in economic recovery in Western Germany. On June 19, 1948, the German Central Bank initiated a currency reform which essentially severed all monetary ties with the East. This reform abolished the old German currency, the Reich mark, and set up a program to immediately replace it with strictly a West Germany currency, the Deutschmark. West Germany would become monetarily independent and become the sole recipient of the benefits of the rebuilding effort starting to take place. This was particularly disturbing to the Soviet Union as the new currency was immediately available in the sections of Berlin controlled by the western countries. East Germany, gutted by the Soviets of its industrial capability, would become a second class country, dependent on the Soviet Union for its economic livelihood. That is the last thing the Soviets wanted. It bitterly denounced the move and threatened reprisals in broadcast after broadcast transmitted over the Iron Curtain.

As an initial step, the Soviet Union banned all travel to and from the eastern zone of the city of Berlin. This was an attempt to maintain the validity of the old currency still in use in that part of the city. A few days later all shipping on the local rivers was halted and electric power, supplied by power plants in the Soviet zone, was cut off. Access to fresh food, normally gotten from the surrounding countryside was no longer available. West Berlin was being isolated from the rest of the world.

Ron and Ingrid grew increasingly concerned about the deteriorating situation as Ingrid's father grew even more alarmed. He had already been through two wars and did not want to see a third. The threat of that loomed ever stronger as the days went by.

Ingrid was spending the evening with Ron as Frau Schlegel visited her sister in a nearby village. They had had a pleasant dinner at the Rose, taken a walk around the village, and gone to bed. A loud knock on the front door woke Ron, and he shook his head to get rid of any cobwebs fashioned by the several beers he had that evening. Ingrid was sound asleep.

The loud pounding came again from the front door. Ron quickly got out of bed, threw on some pants and went downstairs to find out what was going on.

"Sir, you have to report to the Flight Operations Desk right away" said the sergeant. "We have a jeep for you outside."

Ron asked what the problem was but the young sergeant could not say. Instead, he urged him to quickly get dressed and get in the waiting vehicle..

"Dear, listen to me," Ron said on his return to the bedroom. "I have to get to the base for some emergency. Stay here tonight, it shouldn't take too long. Sleep late and I'll see you in the morning when I get back."

Ron stooped down and kissed Ingrid on the forehead. She murmured something that he could not understand, rolled over and went back to sleep.

He smiled and gently closed the door and went downstairs to his waiting transportation

Chapter Ten

The Operations room was full of crew members wondering why they had been called out in the middle of the night. Most were upset, but those like Ron, who had been hearing and reading about the declining relationship between the western counties and the Soviet bloc, knew that something serious had happened but exactly what was a mystery. He looked around and found himself an empty chair, sat down, and waited. He looked at the clock on the wall above the briefing podium and the date under it. It was June 26, 1948.

The door alongside the podium opened and the squadron commander marched to the podium. The crew members stood at attention, waiting to hear him speak.

"Gentlemen, take a seat or find a place to get comfortable," the Colonel said sharply. "This is only going to take a minute and then we have to get to work."

"As you know, the western countries have been engaged in a war of words with the Soviet Union and their allies. This harmless war has now turned ugly. No, we have not been attacked, at least not directly, by the Soviet Union. Indirectly, however, the West's resolve toward the strengthening of Germany into an ally is being called to question. Late last night, the Soviet Union imposed a blockade on the citizens of

West Berlin. This means no food, no water, even no electricity as the power plants are in the Soviet sector. All the roads are closed as are the waterways. The Soviets know that they can do this because there was no agreement between the Allies and them on the use of roadways or waterways. However, there was an agreement on air access which the Soviets are weary of violating, as it may lead to military action. They do not want that, and quite frankly, neither do we.

"Our President does not want to show the world that we will not, or cannot, protect the quality of life of the people living in West Berlin. It would show a weakness in the United States and its Allies and embolden the Soviet Union for any future activity. He has decided that we will support the West Berlin people, and we will do it via the air lines that are open to us. Gentlemen, effective immediately, and until further notice, we are all restricted to this air base and will conduct round-the-clock operations to provide for the citizens of West Berlin. Our allies will also be assisting, but I don't need to tell you that we will be doing the bulk of the flying."

"Your crew chiefs are already working to load critical supplies on your planes. The first one should be ready within two hours. I suggest you find a place to rest until then. Meanwhile, the S-1 is securing additional cots and blankets for those of you who reside off base. You may not spend much time in them, but at least it will be someplace to call your own till this is over."

"Gentlemen, we don't know how long this is going to last, but we know that it will last a little longer. This is a crucial time for the West, and we must not fail. I know you will do your best and make us all proud. Operations will now give you what we know about the operation and how we are going to complete it. Please give him your attention."

A Major stepped to the podium and pulled down a map of Germany. Three lanes of approach into West Berlin had been drawn in dark ink. All three lanes started from the Berlin airport, Templehof. One of them ended at Rhein Main. This would be the lane used by his squadron. As the Major droned on, Matthews' mind returned to Ingrid. Ten minutes later, the scraping of chairs woke him from his thoughts.

"Come on," said his co-pilot, "let's go check the plane."

"OK, Mike, let's go."

Despite it being June, the air was a little chilly, and Matthews lifted his fur collar to cover his neck. People were running around like ants at a picnic, scurrying to get some job done or to assist someone else. Tractors pulling large carts filled with food stuffs moved from plane to plane, while soldiers from the infantry battalion stationed on base helped with loading the planes under the watchful eye of the crew chief.

Matthews' crew chief, Sergeant McNamara, stood watch as a tractor pulled alongside his plane and three soldiers jumped down and ran to the cart piled high with food stuffs. Moving quickly, the soldiers formed a line to better off-load the cart. Sergeant McNamara took the bags from the last soldier and skillfully placed it on the deck of the plane, careful to make sure that the plane was loaded so as to maintain a balanced load. Not doing it right the first time would cost additional time in moving things around to make sure the plane was safe to fly.

"Mac, you going to be alright?"

"Yes sir, but you better get some rest. It's going to be a long haul. I'll send someone for you about half an hour before we are ready to go. That'll give you time to file your flight plan and we can leave right after that. I'll take care of this end, Sir."

Ron nodded and he and Mike started walking toward the flight lounge. Two pilots were just leaving the comfort of over-stuffed chairs and they walked over and got themselves comfortable for the short wait till the biggest airlift in history would start for them.

"Sir, Sir?" Mac called as he entered the flight lounge. Ron stirred and slowly opened his eyes. They slowly adjusted to the waning light and Ron could see Sergeant McNamara standing in the doorway the same way he had been doing so for the last three months. The Sergeant never could allow himself the luxury of completely entering the lounge which was set aside for the officer pilots. Instead, he would open the door and call for his pilots. Despite the number of pilots using the lounge for their own sleeping quarters, the Sergeant's thick Irish accent seemed to by-pass those for which it was not intended and zero in on his two pilots, rousting them from whatever dreams they were witnessing and calling them forth to fly another mission.

It had been three months since the Colonel had made his announcement about the airlift. During that time Ron and his crew had flown every day, sometimes twice a day depending on the quickness of the

85

offloading in Berlin and the reloading in Frankfurt. The flight itself was not long, usually taking only 90 minutes to cover the 300 mile distance between the cities. However, sometimes the planes circled Berlin's Templehof airport for another hour waiting for a time to land. Add to that the need to offload 5,000 pounds of payload the C-47 was capable to carrying, and you can add another couple of hours. The first day of flights had resulted in 64 sorties being flown to Berlin delivering about 156 tons of much needed material. Since that time, the number of sorties had steadily increased with additional planes being made available both from the United States and Great Britain.

Ron shook his head and slowly walked over to a table where a pitcher and bucket stood. He reached his hands into the pitcher, feeling the cool water on his fingers, and splashed the liquid on his face, hoping to speed the wakening. He looked over at his co-pilot and saw his partner leaning over, tying his shoes. His mind wandered to Ingrid. He had sent several notes to her, usually one every couple of days, but had not heard anything back from her. Being restricted on base was beginning to annoy him. He missed her and wanted to hold her again. He was worried that something had happened to keep her from communicating with him. He thought back to the Nazi youth and prayed that they had not returned to get revenge. He shuddered at the thought of what they could do to the old man and the helpless girl. He hoped against hope that they were alright.

That thought traveled with him throughout the day's mission.

Chapter Eleven

The Operations Room was the first place the pilots headed upon their return from Berlin. It contained information on the next mission to be flown, the scheduled departure times for the various aircraft, load information, weather, and generally anything the pilots needed to know. Also on the Situation Board was the aircraft status.

Ron had just returned from his last run of the day. It was early evening and the lights of the city had started to come on. He enjoyed flying at night with the stars above fighting for notice with the electric stars below. The radio broke the silence and reminded him of his pilot duties. The runway was a little to his right and he bent his aircraft around a mythical corner to line up with runway lights. He had done this many times before and knew the routine backwards and forward. As pilot, he mostly did the take-offs and landings, letting his co-pilot fly the straight and level part of the flight. He could indulge himself a bit of fantasy during that time and normally wondered about Ingrid and why she had not answered his notes.

The radio screeched into that thought and provided final landing instructions. It was the same as it had been for the last three months and he methodically went about his business, making the final checks with his co-pilot until the wheels lightly settled on the runway and he headed for loading station number 17. Reaching the loading station, Ron feathered the engines and settled the aircraft down for the night, leaving Mac to handle the final preparations for the next loads. He headed to the Operations Room to see what the next day entailed for him. The chilly, damp air surrounded him like a wet blanket.

Ron stared straight at the next day's schedule as though he could not believe it. His aircraft was scheduled for maintenance the next day, nothing serious, just the routine inspection and maintenance which kept the aircraft in the air until the next scheduled maintenance. He knew because of that, he would have the next day off, that is, unless something happened that required him to pilot a different aircraft.

The Operations Officer, the same Major that spoke about the details of the operation when the Colonel first announced it, was talking with a couple of pilots about some recommended changes in the off-loading procedure which would free the airplanes to return for more supplies without having to wait as long as they did now. Ron had to laugh. Some of the ideas were worth discussion, while others seemed like flights of fancy. However, all would be considered, the Major told them and turned back to what he had been doing.

"Major," said Ron. "Can I speak with you for a minute?"

The Major turned around at Ron's question. "Sure," he said.

"Tomorrow my aircraft is set for scheduled maintenance so there is a good chance that I will not be flying that day. It has been three months since we started this operation and a lot of us have not been off this base. Before the operation began, I had become pretty involved with one of the young German girls in the small village where I was staying. You may have read the story of when her father was attacked by some Nazi youths; I was able to stop them from beating him up. We had become pretty close as a family because of that."

"I wrote them several notes and letters since we started this operation but have not heard back from them at all. I am concerned that something may have happened to them and would really like the opportunity to check it out. I was wondering if I could borrow a jeep tomorrow and go to the village to make sure they are alright. I would be back before the second flight begins in case a substitute pilot is needed and, of course, I would be available if a substitute was needed first thing in the morning. This may be the only chance I have as long as this operation continues, which looks like it is going to be going on for a long time."

The Operations Officer thought for a while. Several other pilots had been given permission to visit friends while their plane was being serviced, under the same limitation as being available in case a substitute pilot was needed. The break had been good for them, gave them a chance to do something different and renew friendships that had been abruptly severed.

"Check into the Ops office at 0600 tomorrow morning. The first flight is scheduled to leave at 0700. If you are not needed, you can have the rest of the morning off base. But you need to be back on base by noon for the afternoon flights. Is that understood?"

"Yes sir," Ron said. "And thank you."

The Major nodded and returned to his scheduling as Ron turned and headed to the lounge where his cot was set up. His co-pilot was not there so he headed to the mess hall to get something to eat. There he found Mike and told him about his conversation with Operations. Mike offered to cover for him in case a substitute pilot was needed, but Ron thought that was his responsibility and declined the offer. They ate quietly, each thinking of the possible day of rest they could look forward to and how they would use it.

Ron was looking forward to seeing Ingrid, but was a little skeptical because he had not heard back from her. That would not have been like her at all, he thought. His mind wandered through scenario after scenario, most of them not pleasant and all of them leaving a wondering in his mind.

A good meal and several cups of coffee later, Ron headed back to the lounge. While one half had been modified to make sleeping quarters, or at least bunks lined up in three rows, the other half still had card tables and magazines along with a one-station radio. Several card games were going, some continuations of games started the first week of the airlift. The scores were in the thousands, but all were relative so no one was upset. Good natured kidding still abounded among the pilots, especially the veteran ones who had been in the operation since the beginning. New pilots, wishing to be included but knowing the ritual, sat and listened to the stories, making mental notes, until one of the other older pilots decided to include them in the discussion. Of course, their contribution to the mission was less than the veterans and usually their comments were met with laughter and jeers. Sheepishly, they turned away from the discussion and looked for their fellow new-bees.

Ron had met some of the new pilots, even gotten to know a few of them, their life stories, where they were from, and their women. But tonight was not a night for socializing. He put the friendly patter behind him, and climbed into his bunk. His tired body sank quickly into sleep but his mind kept on going, counting every tick of the clock until the morning would arrive.

Chapter Twelve

The rustling of bodies getting ready for work woke Ron up from his stupor. He had wanted to sleep lightly lest his tired body take over and cause him to sleep through his 0600 appointment. However, he had slept longer than he wanted and left himself just enough time to shave, get changed, and head over to the Operations Center. The final group of pilots entered the room and he joined them just as the door was closing. Standing in the back of the room he peered over and around the other pilots straining to see the Pilot Status Board which hung in the front of the room between the Aircraft Status Board and the flight headings for the next scheduled flight.

A Captain, the Assistant Operations Officer, began his briefing by identifying the aircraft which would be used for the morning's delivery. Each aircraft tail number was read out loud and its condition stated as green, yellow, or red. If green, the aircraft was ready to go, having been loaded during the night and waiting for its crew. If yellow, the aircraft was scheduled to go, but was not yet ready for some reason; usually because there was a problem with the loading of the supplies and extra time was needed. If red, the aircraft was not available due to routine maintenance or a maintenance problem which had cropped up and needed fixing before the plane could fly. Ron's plane tail number was matched with a red sticker indicating that his plane would not be used today. That was a good sign.

While the Captain was talking, the Operations Sergeant would update the flight boards as new information became available. In just the short time that the Captain went over the weather report and the routes to Berlin, several more aircraft had moved from yellow to green. More planes for more supplies.

But Ron's interest lay elsewhere. The Pilot Status Board drew all his attention. All the names of the pilots and co-pilots scheduled to fly that day were neatly written in chalk on the board. Beside each name, like on the Aircraft Status Board, was a colored sticker. The same system as used on the Aircraft Status Board was used for the pilot's status: red, green, and yellow. Ron glared intently at the Pilot Board, his mind seeking to force nothing but green on the board. And in all cases but one, the stickers were green. Ron's heart froze as he saw the Operations Sergeant change one sticker from green to yellow....Tom Burgess.

"But," he thought, "I saw Tom get up this morning and head out before I did." He looked around to find him, but with so many people in the room, it was impossible to see them all. He lowered his head, clenched his lips, and swore under his breath.

"Damn," he said.

A breath of chilly morning air entered the room causing everyone to turn and see what had caused the sudden change in temperature. Tom Burgess had entered the room and was making his way to the Operations Officer, waving a piece of paper in front of him. He handed it to the Major and turned, seeing his co-pilot who waved and directed him over to the corner where he stood.

The Major read the paper, called the Sergeant over and handed it to him. The Sergeant looked at the paper, moved to the Pilot Status Board and removed the yellow sticker next to Tom Burgess's name. He replaced it with a green sticker and a sigh involuntarily escaped from Ron's lips. It must have been louder than he thought as several friends who knew he was looking for the day off, looked at Ron and chuckled.

He looked at them with a smile in his eyes, raised both his arms as to say "Whatever" and slowly made his way out of the Operations Center to find a hot cup of coffee. He would have a little breakfast, and then get with the Major to get the jeep. His morning was looking pretty good so far, but he still wondered what would lie ahead of him at the village. But first things first. The coffee smelled real good.

The ride to the village seemed to take forever. The chilly morning air seemed to whip across his face despite the presence of a windshield and canvas top and sides. Jeeps were not made to be very protective from the climate. They were basic transportation, requiring little maintenance and designed to go almost anywhere. And they fulfilled their function very well. But they didn't afford any forms of luxury. In fact, they did not even have a key. There was only an ignition switch which you turned on and then stepped on the starter switch which caused the engine to turn over. Since anyone could get in and start one up, security was maintained by a length of heavy chain and a padlock. The chain did not stop the engine from being started, but it was thread through the steering wheel and the driver's seat in such a manner as to restrict the steering wheel's turning. The result, a moving jeep which could not be steered. As such, more of a liability than an asset and thus usually left alone.

As Ron entered the village which he had left over three months ago, he noticed that several houses had been boarded up and appeared to be vacant. Turning the corner onto the street that the zum Rose stood, he noticed that the gasthaus was, itself, boarded up. A note on a thick piece of paper carelessly hung from the boarded entrance. Words in German took up the space on the paper.

Ron stopped the jeep, put it in neutral and set the parking brake. He got out of the vehicle and walked over to the now boarded entrance and tried to read the words on the sign to no avail. Whatever little German he had learned had flitted away over the past three months and he was at a loss. He pulled the note off the boards, climbed into the jeep, and slowly drove to his old room, hoping Frau Schlegel would be there. To his delight, there were no boards across the front door and a tiny light escaped from the front window through the wooden curtains.

He softly knocked on the front door and breathed a sigh of relief as he heard the inner locks being opened. The door edged open a fraction, and Ron could see the familiar eyes of Frau Schlegel. She immediately recognized him and gleefully opened the door and welcomed him inside and led him to the parlor. She sat and waited for him to speak.

"Frau Schlegel, how are you?" he asked.

She nodded her head. "Gut," she said. "A little…," she paused looking for the right English word. "Scared? Frightened," she said with a question in her voice.

Ron nodded his head in understanding. Having just escaped from a long war, much of the German populace was afraid that the situation with the Berlin airlift was just a prelude to another war, this one between Russia and the United States but fought on German territory. Uncertain where it was heading, they cautiously lived each day in the hopes of seeing the next. It was a scary time in Germany and Frau Schlegel was typical of the population living in it.

Ron reached into his overcoat and pulled out the sign taken from zum Rose. Frau Schlegel recognized it immediately and began to talk excitedly about its contents. Ron had to slow her down so that he could understand what she was saying. Even speaking slowly, he still had trouble understanding all she was saying.

Frau Schlegel slowly composed herself and began to explain to Ron that Herr Kurtz and his daughter, Ingrid had left the village. Like many Germans, herself included, Herr Kurtz was afraid that the situation between the two super powers would further disintegrate, resulting in another war. He wanted to be out of the middle of it, so he closed his restaurant and, with his daughter, moved to stay with some friends on the French border. He had told Frau Schlegel that he would return when things eased up a bit and there was less chance of a war.

Ron remembered his discussions with Herr Kurtz about his injury in World War I, the death of his wife,

Ingrid's mother, and the going through of a second war. He remembered the elder saying that he was not about to be in the middle of a third one. He had done his duty, felt his pain, and would move with his daughter rather than taking a chance of being caught in the middle of another conflict. Fearing that was the case, he had escaped to what he thought was a safer place and had taken his daughter with him.

Tears welled up in Ron's eyes as he thought about never seeing Ingrid again.

Frau Schlegel leaned over and patted his arm, knowing what he was thinking. She reached into her pocket and pushed a bundle of paper into his hand.

"Ingrid," she whispered.

Chapter Thirteen

My Dearest Ron,

*I*f you get this, then you know that my father and
I have moved away and are staying with some
friends near the French border. The stress and
strain on my father as a result of the recent
conflict between the United States and Russia was too
much. He was constantly staring out the windows and
mumbling of tanks and soldiers coming. Villagers
stopped coming to the restaurant because of that and
he was becoming the village joke. I could not bear to
see him like that. When he suggested that we moved
further west for a while, I knew that I had to do that,
for his health, both mentally and physically.

*I gave Frau Schlegel several notes to give to you
before we left, in case you came back to your room to
get some things. However, I guess that never
happened. When I gave her this note, she still had the
other three in her apron pocket. I asked her to throw
them away as this is the only important one now.*

*Dear Ron, I have missed you and missed being
with you. You broke through my walls, opened my
eyes to what life has to offer, and made me
understand that if I want to get anything out of this
life, I have to live it, not just live in it. Who I am is as
much about you as it is about me. You have taught me
how to love, how to experience life and learn from
that experience. You have taught me how not to be*

afraid, to look each situation straight ahead, and do what I think is right. You have taught me that strength is not muscle, but determination; not resentfulness, but resolve; not religion, but faith; not lust, but love. What strength I have has been nurtured by you, to help make me what I am today.

Ron, I love you. I knew that the evening you walked into the gasthaus but was afraid to admit it. That is, until that evening we returned from the wine fest. Having spent all day with you was like spending the day in your soul and seeing what made you Ron. Not Ronald, not Ronnie, but Ron. And it thrilled me to no end.

Ron, I don't know when we will see each other again, or if we will. I want the former and fear the latter. But the future doesn't open up for me, and I don't know what will happen. I do know that when this is over, we will return to the village and re-open the gasthaus and I will search the whole country for you. I pray to God that I will find you!

I have put in this note a picture of us taken during one of our trips. I hope you like it. I have a copy also and will hold onto it forever. If nothing else, I will cherish this pictures of the two of us, as my first love, and the one that taught me that love is not changing oneself to please the other, but rather giving of oneself as is, and accepting the other person for what they are. That is the only way I can love.

Ron, please take care of yourself. I hope, from the bottom of my heart, that we will rejoin our lives and live them together as long as possible. But if that is not to be, then I say "Thank You" for giving me mine,

for loving me as I am, and for teaching me that love and life may be one and the same.
Love,
Ingrid.

Chapter Fourteen

The drive back to the airbase was automatic. His mind raced one way, then another, then another until, if one could look inside it, one would see a ball of twine with strands running each and every way, a different strand for each thought. The only intrusion to this mental abyss was the ragged hum of the tires on the cobblestones, their soulful sound a dirge, a fitting accompaniment to the deep morass through which his mind was struggling to see, to understand, and finally, to escape.

The escape came in the form of an MP checking identification cards at the airbase gate. He showed his and was quickly waved through, his thoughts slowly returning to the task at hand but his memory firmly ensconced within the words and picture which filled his jacket pocket.

His world was waiting outside those gates and he so wanted to return to it.

Chapter Fifteen

The monthly calendar had turned six more pages, and the green coat worn by the German countryside had been replaced with a white mantel of fresh snow. Six months had passed since his empty return from the village, six months of almost daily flying back and forth to Berlin. While each flight seemed to grow longer and longer, the cumulative effect of the airlift seemed to have accelerated the passage of time. No longer did he fly the C-47. It had been replaced by the larger and faster C-54, a cargo plane capable of carrying more tonnage at a faster rate, thus increasing the flow of needed supplies into the war-torn city.

The C-54 was a four engine aircraft powered by Pratt and Whitney R-2000-7 engines with 1350 horsepower each. While its maximum speed was only 35 miles per hour faster than the C-4 and its ceiling actually less than the C-47, its payload was far greater. The C-47 had a payload of about 5000 pounds. The C-54, known as the "Skymaster" could carry almost 20,000 pounds of cargo, making it 4 times as efficient with no loss in speed and a 400 mile advantage in range. Thus it could carry more and fly further between refueling operations adding considerably to the capability of the air operations.

British and French planes now flew alongside the American's and a new airfield in the French sector of Berlin called Tegel was opened to add to the receiving capability in Berlin The other airports were insufficient to sustain the hundreds of flights arriving daily with the much-needed supplies for the city residents. Besides food stuff, coal was the most needed commodity during this time of the year. The German winter could be brutal, the cold wind sweeping down from the Russian steppes, carrying wet snow and dumping it on the impoverished city. Without the coal, the city would cease to function and its residents would be forced to scrounge the countryside for anything that would burn. Before the arrival of the early shipments of coal, complete buildings in the evening would be missing sections in the morning as the shivering population sought to keep itself warm. The continuous arrival of the coal seemed to stop that, though occasionally a building would collapse and the local populace would swarm over it like ants at a picnic, looking for anything that could provide the needed warmth.

Ron's C-54 was approaching his second landing of the day into Templehof. This airfield had been the main airfield in Berlin, and almost reduced to ruins during the bombing runs into the city. Upon its capture, troops had found beneath its runways an aircraft factory, completely capable of building fighter planes for the Luftwaffe. These fighter planes were discovered standing in various stages of completion, lined up like the soldiers they were destined to become. Some were mere shells of their intended selves, other complete with wings and armament, lacking only the ammunition to begin their deadly task. An elevator leading to one of the hangers above the ground, allowed the completed plane to

103

reach the surface of the airfield and join the war. The factory was no longer in operation, rather it lay there as a grim reminder of the inventiveness of the Nazi regime and its unfulfilled thirst for conquest in the name of the German people, the same ones that were now being fed and warmed by the Third Reich's sworn enemies.

The radio cackled as the tower sought to make some sense of the swarming planes and carefully guide them to a safe landing.

"C827, come to heading 060," Ron heard through his earphones.

"Roger," he replied, "turning to heading 060."

The huge cargo plane slowly turned to the right, its left wing reaching for the sky while the right wing pointed to the ground below. Ron could see two planes in front of him, both on the same heading, the furthest being two miles in front and the second, half that distance. The lead plane already had his landing gear down and was on final approach. The one closest to Ron had opened his landing gear doors and he could see the black wheels slowly emerge from their den, as though stretching to wake up and move on.

It always amazed Ron landing at Templehof. The whole thrust of the operation was to unload the cargo as fast as possible and head back for more. Little time was wasted in taxiing upon landing, and while the plane was slowed down upon touchdown, it was quickly led by a "follow me" vehicle to the nearest unloading stations. These vehicles were waiting near the end of the runway, somewhat akin to the racetrack horses waiting for the thoroughbreds to enter the track so they can lead them in their warm-up. The vehicles, and there were usually 8 or 10 of them, each with at least two airmen, sometimes three, maneuvered in front of the still moving planes and guided them to their destination where troops stood ready to unload their valuable cargo and speed it into the city. Upon completion, the vehicle led the plane back to the cue of others waiting to take off, then sped back to the pick-up area for the next one. Unless there was a problem, the planes rarely even turned off their engines; that was how fast the unloading went.

Ron judged the distance to the runway, turned on the landing lights and flipped the landing gear switch to set up for the landing. He heard the flaps open, and the gears begin to lower the wheels into a locked position. The right gear locked into position indicated by a green light on the console, but the left gear remained red.

"Damn," he said. "Mac, check the left gear will you?"

The crew chief unstrapped himself from his seat and peered out the left side window.

"Looks like it's stuck, Sir," he said into the intercom. "It's about a third of the way down."

Ron jiggled the toggle switch, hoping that the intermittent current would cause the wheels to drop.

"Anything now?" he asked.

"Nope, still hanging."

There was a standard procedure for something like this and Ron knew what had to be done.

"Templehof Tower, this is C827. Experiencing gear problems. Request permission to exit landing pattern and take up holding position until resolved."

"C827, understand. Take up the northern holding position and report status when able."

"Templehof Tower, this is C827. Roger, leaving landing pattern and moving to northern holding pattern. Will report status when determined."

"Roger, C827. Good luck."

Ron slowly banked the loaded plane to the left and proceeded to take up a circular pattern north of the city. Knowing that problems will surely crop up, the Operations folks had established a holding sector just north of the city. Aircraft experiencing any type of problem which precluded it from landing were instructed to that position which removed them from the traffic flow and gave them the opportunity to resolve the problem. Once resolved, they rejoined the landing pattern and completed their mission. If not resolved, they were not allowed to land in Berlin but rather instructed to return to their own base, the thought being that if there was a problem with the landing, better to have one of the departure airfields unusable than one of the two airfields in Berlin closed down.

Ron checked his fuel gauges and saw that fuel was not a problem. Having fueled prior to his last departure, they showed enough fuel to last several hours. A quick glance over the other instruments indicated that with the exception of the reluctant wheel all else was green. He glanced over to his co-pilot who made a circular motion with his hand. Ron nodded and switched on his intercom.

"Mac, get out the hand-crank and try and get it down with that."

106

Mac looked up at the pilot, gave him a thumbs up and proceeded to get the hand-crank from its storage locker. The crank was much like that used for changing a car tire. It was L-shaped, with a lug on one end which fit into the landing wheel gear. Turning the other end, the lug rotated the gear, manually forcing the wheel down until it clicked into place, locking it and precluding its collapse upon touching down.

With the hand-crank in place, Mac tried to turn the gear, lowering the wheel. As much as he tried, the wheel would not descend. Again and again he tried, but each time to no avail.

"Sir, it's not turning. Did you disengage the electric motor?"

"You dumb jerk," Ron thought of himself as he reached for the fuse to disengage the motor which raised and lowered the gear. Without doing that, the motor acted as a brake to the wheel, and Mac could have used a tank to turn the crank and it still would have not worked.

"Sorry, Mac. Try it now."

The crew chief returned to the hand-crank and applied pressure. Slowly but surely, the crank turned and he could see the wheel begin to appear below the wing. The rush of the wind against the wheel made it tough, but about five minutes later the wheel was down and locked.

"Way to go, Mac," said Ron when he saw the red light turn green. "Way to go."

"Templehof Tower, this is C827. Incident resolved. Ready to resume approach for landing."

"Roger C827, come to heading 290 till you cross the river, then assume heading of 180."

Ron knew the flight route would take him west of the city, then turn south toward the long line of planes heading to the beleaguered city. The tower would try to fit him into the pattern by slowing down other planes to make room, then slide him into the now vacant airspace.

"Roger Templehof, heading 290. Request maintenance assistance upon landing and unloading for hanging left wheel. Required hand crank to set and lock into position."

"Roger C827. Will advise ground control, lead vehicle and maintenance to expect your arrival."

Reaching the river, Ron banked the plane to the left and headed south. As expected, he soon saw several planes heading almost perpendicular to his route. The tower skillfully guided him between two other C-54s and he resumed his approach routine, going through the same checklist he had done a hundred times.

The landing was smooth, the apprehension they all experienced turned out to be unnecessary. Instead of the normal lead vehicle, a jeep with flashing red lights maneuvered in front of him and led him first to the unloading area where fifteen minutes later he was done, then to the maintenance hangar where a group of mechanics were waiting to identify and solve the problem. The ground guide led him to a designated spot and signaled to Ron to stop the engines. With a flutter, the huge propellers came to a halt.

The maintenance crew scrambled aboard as Ron and his crew looked for a cup of coffee. The Army Air Corps flew on coffee.

Chapter Sixteen

A couple of hours later Mac found the pilots in the mess hall still drinking the dark coffee and talking with other pilots from Britain and France. Their countries were contributing to the airlift and while most of the flights were undertaken by the United States, every little bit was appreciated. The pilots regardless of their nationality all had the same persona, the swag of men on a mission, the rescue of the free world from the clutches of Ivan. They were united in their mission and determined to complete it as best they could.

"Sir, we should be ready to go in about ten minutes," said Mac as he walked up to the two American pilots seated at the long table.

Ron looked up and nodded as he took one last sip. Ron liked Mac. He could be relied upon to get things done. He was the doer of the trio who saw that the needs of the two officers were taken care of, whatever that might be. Ron and Jack relied on Mac to handle the details. Jack, in turn, would handle the flight plans, maintenance scheduling, and logistics associated with the aircraft. He and Mac worked well together and Ron, the overseer, the big-picture guy, kept them focused and headed in the right direction. Ron was the rudder of a ship, guiding the crew to achieve success after success. Jack kept the oars moving, and Mac made sure the other two had the tools they needed to do their jobs. It worked well.

The two pilots shook the hands of their counterparts and left the mess hall. Passing through the door, they could see the last of the mechanics exiting the side hatches of their plane. Mac was handing down the mechanics' tool chests and looked up as he saw the two pilots approaching. He reached down to give each a hand up the ladder and closed the hatch behind them as they walked to the front of the aircraft.

"The problem with the gear was a relay switch that went bad," Mac said. "They replaced the switch and tested it. It should be good to go. Meanwhile, I had them top off the tanks since we had the time. Should be enough for another couple of runs before more is needed."

"Mac was always thinking ahead" thought Ron. "He could have sat around waiting for the mechanics do their job, but instead he had the plane refueled to ensure continued operations without having to stop again. Good job."

Ron settled himself into the pilot's seat leaving the canvas strap loose until they reached the number one take-off spot. He looked over at Jack who was busy going through the check list prior to take-off. Some of the items could be checked by one pilot and Jack was always ahead of the game when it came to that. Other items needed to be checked by both of the pilots, and Jack's part was usually done by the time that he got settled in his seat.

The engines started smoothly, one at a time, until all four were humming sweetly. All the gauges showed green except the brake and as Ron slowly released it and pushed forward on the throttles, the red turned green and the steel Skymaster slowly lumbered toward the line of planes waiting to get airborne. Following instructions from ground control, he settled his plane behind an older C-47 and waited his turn.

Fifteen minutes later Ron tightened his shoulder straps, made a right turn and lined up down the center of the runway.

"C827, you are cleared for take-off. See you next time."

"Roger, Templehof tower, C827 rolling."

The C-54 slowly accelerated down the runway, smoothly left the confines of the earth and took its place among the noisy metal flock headed to reload and return at a later time.

The flight was short but hampered by a line of clouds which reduced the visibility. While that would normally not have been a problem, with so many planes in the air the two pilots were constantly twisting and turning heads to avoid bumping into something. Even Mac was kept busy, moving from one side of the aircraft to the other, trying to provide another set of eyes.

The plane rumbled through the sky at about 250 miles per hour, below its maximum speed but a comfortable cruising speed. At the designated point, Ron began his descent into Rhein Main. The plane buffered a little as it sliced through the clouds but suddenly broke free and into the clear. Ron could see the airfield about 30 miles ahead, He slowed the aircraft and contacted the tower.

"Rhein Main tower, this is C827 requesting permission to land."

"Roger C827, we have you in sight. Distance is 25 miles, descend to 5000 feet and wait further instructions."

Ron looked over at Jack who was again going through the landing checklist. He glanced at the panel and saw that all was in order. In preparation for the final approach he switched on the landing lights and toggled the landing gear switch. He could feel the wheel wells open and the grinding of the gears as they lowered the rubber wheels into position. Unlike the C-47, the C-54 had a nose wheel. Ron had had to get used to that during the transition from the old C-47. During the first landing of the C-54 he had expected the rear of the aircraft to slowly sink to the concrete. When the aircraft started to lean forward he momentarily panicked and the instructor pilot had laughed, explaining that almost all of the transition pilots did the same thing. It was second nature now.

The red light blinked on the control panel and its flashing caught both Ron and Jack at the same time. It was the left landing gear. Again.

"Damn," thought Ron. "Here we go again. Mac, check it out again, will you?"

"Looks like the same thing, Skipper. I'll get the crank."

Ron nodded in agreement and remembering the last time, reached over to disengage the electric motor that, for the second time, had failed to do its job. He glanced over his shoulder and gave his crew chief the thumbs up indicating that he could go about his task.

Mac set up the hand crank and slowly started to move the left gear down into position. The wheel reluctantly emerged from its comfortable den and moved into position.

"C827 this is Rhein Main tower. Descend to 2000feet and take up visual approach. You are cleared for landing."

"Rhein Main tower, C827 cleared for landing."

Ron nudged the nose of the plane downward, the propellers pulling the steel cylinder through the air toward the concrete ribbon straight ahead. Turbulence from the ground shook the plane as it descended, sometimes severely shaking the pilots.

Ron looked over his shoulder at Mac who was still trying to lower the wheel. He struggled against both the wind racing against the wheel and the bouncing of the aircraft. Unsteadily, he nevertheless kept turning the crank until Ron indicated that the panel light had turned green. Mac stowed away the crank, cursing the mechanics who had failed to do their job. He swore he would give them a piece of his mind the next time he was in Berlin. Still being bounced around, he managed to get to his seat and strap himself in and waited for the landing.

Ron aimed the silver bird to touch down about one-third of the way down the runway. Keeping the nose of the aircraft up, the right wheel touches first, screeching as it starts to rotate and roll. The left side of the aircraft settles shortly thereafter and the nose wheel begins its smooth rotation to earth.

Suddenly the left side of the aircraft lurches and squeals to the concrete.

And all hell breaks loose.

Chapter Seventeen

The three men in the rushing cylinder felt before they knew that something was wrong. As the left wing settled down to the horizontal, there was a loud crack out the left window. Ron turned quickly to the left to see what it was while Jack steadfastly kept his eyes on the runway, his hands securely around the wheel waiting for the next thing. Mac was secure in the rear of the aircraft heard it also, his head straining to see out the left window.

It was Mac who saw it first.

"Sir, left gear is…."

Before he could finish his sentence, both pilots understood what had happened. While the light on the console had turned green indicated that the left wheel had been lowered and locked in place, in fact that was not the case. The wheel had failed to lock, and the green light had mistakenly indicated a locked gear. The left wing, the air still flowing over its curved silhouette, remained horizontal to the runway, but Ron knew that if he slowed down, the wing would drop, come in contact with the runway, and the plane would careen down the concrete.

Without even thinking, he shoved the throttles forward and the four Pratt and Whitney engines roared in protest. The runway quickly sped underneath the crippled plane and Ron realized that he had to make a choice. If he kept on going at the speed he was going, he would quickly run out of runway and barrel head first into an unfinished building at the end of the pavement. There was just not enough left of the concrete ribbon to allow the plane to gain sufficient speed to clear the building. That was apparent.

The alternative was to break the plane, let the wing sag to the ground, and hope to withstand the resulting spin. He had seen it before, the spinning propellers clawing at the concrete as though trying to dig themselves a hole. The tips of the blades broke off or bent upward, some staying stuck in the concrete, some flying through the air like an airborne guillotine, and some just bent as if to say this is the best I can do.

"Hang on, guys...going to bring it to a stop, someplace."

Ron brought the throttles all the way back to reverse, hoping to bring the plane to a halt before the end of the runway. As he did so he stomped on the brake, locking the nose wheel and the one wing wheel till they smoked. Alternating between applying the brakes and backing off of them, he hoped to stop the plane without the risk of fire. He fought the nose wheel, struggling to turn right as the right brake took hold, but nothing slowed the left side of the aircraft. Jack joined him in trying to keep the nose wheel straight, and between the two of them they physically stopped the plane from spinning to the right.

To his left, Ron could see the left wing begin to sag, the propeller getting dangerously close to the ground. But he had no choice; the end of the runway was starring him right in the face.

He heard the sirens of the emergency vehicles and looked up to see them heading in his direction from the end of the runway he was approaching. He had always wondered why they were at either end of the runway, but now understood that accidents usually took place at either end, not in the middle. By being at the end, they were able to reach the scene that much quicker. And the difference between life and death could be a matter of seconds.

The sounds of the sirens were suddenly overridden by the left propeller screeching across the concrete, following quickly by the second. Blades of the shattered first propeller flew through the air, then cart-wheeled along the grass until falling over as though a result of exhaustion. By the time the blades of the second propeller hit, the wing tip had already been ripped off and liquid was flowing from the wing like olive oil over a salad. But this was not olive oil, but rather highly flammable aviation fuel. Ron watched in horror as the deadly liquid spewed out, but even more so as the plane was now turning in its direction on what was now the remains of the left wing. With nothing to do but wait, he closed his eyes and prayed.

With nothing to support the left wing, it hit the ground taking with it the rear of the airplane. Mac was sitting about two-thirds down the empty cargo compartment realizing that what was to happen was out of his hands. He reached up and tightened his straps one last time just as the fuselage began to crack immediately to his left, between him and the cockpit. Within seconds he was riding in a tail section completely separated from the rest of the aircraft.

Having no wheels and forced forward by its own momentum, the tail section slid forward and to the right of the front of the plane. He saw both pilots look at him when he passed, but that became a quick memory as the cockpit rotated to the left, toward the leaking fuel while the rear of the plane escaped the harshness of the concrete and settled into the welcome softness of the grass infield and came to a stop.

Mac waited for a fraction of a second, then knew that he had to get out of the plane in case of fire. Releasing his harness, he quickly moved to the gaping hole where the cockpit had been and jumped down onto the grass. Without hesitation, he ran around the tail section to see the situation of the two pilots.

It was not good.

The cockpit had almost made a 180 degree turn, facing in the opposite direction from where it had landed a couple of minutes ago. The liquid fuel continued to flow out of the wing tanks and the nose had settled into a big puddle. The emergency vehicles were scurrying across the field as quickly as possible, ambulances, fire engines, and other emergency vehicles all intent on reaching the crew before the unthinkable happened. Small grass fires dotted the scene, caused by the metal scraping on the concrete, sending sparks into the grass and causing the flare-ups.

Mac realized the danger, and ran as fast as he could to the cockpit, now laying like a dead bird, its wings broken and its body lying in ruins. Because of his proximity to the cockpit, he was the first person there, the emergency crews roaring across the field but slowed by the unevenness of the terrain. First that is, except for one small brush fire that seemed to be racing him to the two pilots. They both reached the wounded aircraft at the same time.

The small fire reached a puddle of the aviation fuel about the same time that Mac reached the open end of the cockpit. The puddle burst into a solid wall of flame and quickly moved toward the cockpit. Mac felt the rush of hot air, but instead of hesitating this only made him move faster. Jumping into the back of the plane, he darted through the miles of wiring hanging from the fuselage. As he moved forward he could see the fire moving closer to the plane through the windows, or at least what used to be the windows. Reaching the cockpit, he struggled to open the jammed door finally tearing it off its hinges to get inside. The inside was a total disaster, its neatly planned interior strewn about like an unsupervised kindergarten class, broken instruments dangling by their wires, glass all over, and the steering controls buckled under the weight of the pilots as they were thrust forward upon them. The two pilots slumped over the controls.

A huge wall of fire flamed up outside of the cockpit and startled the crew chief. He made it to Jack first, and tried to move him, but there was no movement. He looked at the co-pilot and realized that he was dead, the result of a broken neck suffered in the crash. Not hesitating, he moved to Ron to check him out. The flame got closer to the window and through it he could see the fire trucks begin to try and douse the fire. But it had gotten a good head start, and there was still more fuel in the other tanks in the broken plane, ready to explode as if on command.

Mac reached for Ron and squeezed his hand. His reward was a small squeeze in return and a slight movement of his arm. Not hesitating, Mac reached for his survivor knife and cut away the straps holding the pilot to his chair. Without the support, Ron lurched forward only to be caught by the burly hands of the crew chief. Knowing the risk of moving an injured man, but also knowing that sure death waited for both of them if they stayed there much longer, Mac carefully pulled Ron out of his seat, put his hands under the pilot's arms and across his chest and dragged him out of the cockpit to what remained of the body of the aircraft. Once out of the cockpit, he carefully lifted the pilot over his shoulder and rapidly moved to the open end. Rescuers swarmed toward them, reaching up to grab the pilot and lower him on a stretcher, then reaching for Mac to help him out of the fuselage. Already Ron had been placed in an ambulance which quickly started for the hospital. As Mac jumped down from what remained of the plane, a blast of flame and hot air pushed him and his helpers to the ground. Reacting more than knowing, they quickly got up and ran as fast as they could away from the wreckage. As the flames reached the remaining fuel, the plane erupted in flames turning the once proud Skymaster into a twisted mass of charred metal.

Chapter Eighteen

The dreariness of the winter season was slowly stealing out the back door of the New Year as spring peaked around the corner, waiting to take its place. The small hospital room, its singular window overlooking a grass park, provided little comfort for its occupant. A small metal hospital bed occupied the wall opposite the window, flanked by the obligatory hospital instruments on one side and the ever-present fluid stand on the other. From the bag hanging on the stand ran a plastic tube, the other end of which disappeared under a gauze bandage taped on the patient's arm. Liquid dripped from the bag, slowly made its way down the tube and joined its carrier in disappearing under the bandage. The fluid carried the nutrients needed by the patient to keep him alive, his ability to eat normal food completely inoperative due to the coma which had controlled his life since the accident. For three months Ron Matthews had been drifting in and out of a coma, unaware of what was happening or where he was. His last recollection was being lifted out of his seat by a set of big, strong hands, and manhandled out of the aircraft to a waiting ambulance. Everything between then and now was a virtual blank.

Ron Matthews had no idea how lucky he was to be alive. The crash that had killed his co-pilot had knocked him unconscious, broken a couple of ribs, and fractured his right leg. If it had not been for his crew chief, those injuries would not have mattered for Ron would have perished in the flaming inferno that was left of his plane. But Mac had somehow survived the crash with enough strength left to carry the wounded pilot out of the plane before it burst into flames. Mac had saved his life, he would later learn.

From the plane, Matthews was transported to the base hospital. But the facilities there were insufficient to care for the severely traumatized pilot and he was transferred to the civilian facility in Frankfurt, a much more modern and up-to-date facility which would provide better care for him. Upon his arrival there, he was still unconscious and needed assistance in breathing. It took a couple of days to get him stabilized before being transferred to the States. He was admitted to Walter Reed Army Hospital in NW Washington DC and settled into one of the critical care rooms. That was three months ago.

Ruth Matthews had spent the better part of those three months in this room, switching occasionally with her husband when she needed a break from the routine. A telegram personally delivered by an Army Lieutenant had informed her and her husband of the accident and made arrangements for their travel to Washington DC from their home in New Jersey to be with their son. Their arrival at Union Station was met with a sedan which sped them to the hospital to see Ron..

Ruth and her husband Paul had checked into the little guest house on the hospital grounds in hopes of only staying a couple of days. But as the days wore on, Paul had to return to his hardware store in New

Brunswick. He was the only one working it, though his brother would cover for him in the case of an emergency. However, there was no way he could ask his brother to cover for weeks which turned into months, especially with no end in sight. The couple had decided that Ruth would stay at the hospital while Paul would return home, returning every couple of weeks on the weekend when he could close the store and join his wife. She looked at her watch, then down at her sleeping son who had laid there all this time without moving, then out the window, saying a little prayer to whoever would listen.

The door to the hospital room launched open and the old, gray-haired nurse strode purposely to her task. Alongside the bed, she checked to make sure the IV was still running as set, that there were no changes in any of the other instruments which would cause her an alarm, and finally took the pulse of the patient in such a way as to convince Ruth that it really didn't matter if there was one there or not. She was just doing her job. She pressed her finger into the patient's wrist and watched her watch as the second hand made its obligatory stroll through time. After fifteen seconds, she lowered the wrist to the bed and noted the pulse rate on the bedside clipboard containing all the other pertinent information on the condition of the pilot. She paused for a moment, settled the clipboard into position, looked at Ruth, then exited the room without a word. Ruth shrugged and settled into one of the chairs and waited for time to pass slowly.

A couple of minutes later the nurse reentered the room and motioned for Ruth to follow her. Quizzically, she stood up, put her book on the chair and hesitantly followed the nurse out of the room and into the general waiting room near the nurses' station.

"Please wait here for a minute, Mrs. Matthews," she said, "the doctor wants to examine your son."

As she sat down, her husband rounded the corner heading to his son's room.

"Paul," said Ruth. "Wait. Come here."

Paul stopped abruptly, wondering who had called him and why. He looked around and saw Ruth now standing in the general waiting room, her face a big question mark.

"Is everything ok?" he asked.

"I don't know. The nurse came in as usual, took the vital signs and left. A couple of minutes later she asked me to wait here because the doctor wanted to examine Ron. I have been here about twenty minutes but don't know what is going on."

They worriedly chatted about the situation and wondered what it could mean. Meanwhile, they could see more and more of the hospital staff going into their son's room, some bringing equipment, some taking it out. There was a sense of purpose around their rush to get something done, a sense that had slowly disappeared over time as the comatose patient failed to respond to any stimuli. Something was happening.

Thirty minutes passed, then forty-five, then an hour. Meanwhile Ruth and Paul alternately sat down and then got up and paced the floor, looking down the hall trying to fathom what was happening.

About an hour and a half passed, and the train of nurses and doctors into and out of their son's room seemed to have ended. Finally, the doctor who had

123

been treating Ron emerged from the hospital room, looked for the couple and seeing them, moved quickly in their direction.

Major Evanston had been treating Ron since his arrival at Walter Reed. He was an expert of sorts on comatose cases, having studied that in med school and during the War. He had experienced many cases due to shell shock or the like. His manner was not gruff, but neither was it condescending. He told you the way things were, not necessarily what you wanted to hear.

Their first meeting with the doctor, upon Ron's arrival, had been anything but hopeful. Having seen many cases like this, he prepped them for the worse, that most of the patients either never awoke and thus passed away without awakening, or if they did come out of the coma, were never the same as a result of little or no blood going to the head and brain. It was important, he told them, to keep on top of all medical signs as the smallest one could be an indication of something different happening.

Major Evanston reached the Matthews, stretched out his hand to greet each of them, and then asked that they be seated.

Without taking their eyes off of the doctor, Ruth and Paul sat down and waited.

"We have had somewhat of a breakthrough," he said. "The nurse noticed an increase in the pulse rate which would indicate additional blood getting to the brain. That was, and is a good sign. We just spent the last hour going through a battery of tests to see where Ron stands in regard to regaining his full facilities. Unfortunately, while some of the test showed positive results, others did not. It could be that those that did not were just too far upstream and he has not progressed that far yet, and we hope that is the case. Or, he will never progress that far. At this point we just don't know."

Paul and Ruth rushed to ask their questions, but the doctor put up his hand.

"What we do know," he said, "is that your son has pulled out of his coma and is responding to stimuli, albeit in a small way, but he is responding. His arm moved when we pricked it with a tiny needle, his knee jerked when stimulated, and most importantly," the doctor hesitated," he opened his eyes."

Ruth gasped and caught her breath at the same time. She reached over and grabbed her husband's arm, waiting for the next piece of news.

"While he did not speak," the doctor continued, "He did seem to recognize where he was and instead of staring straight ahead, turned his head to look out the window. Without giving you false hope, we may have turned the corner."

Ruth openly sobbed into her hands as Paul put his arm around her shoulder. The Major leaned forward and placed his hands on theirs.

"Let's go see him," he whispered.

Chapter Nineteen

The two-story wooden framed house stood a little back from the street, its porch stretching all the way across the front of the house, the porch roof held up by neatly painted white poles which broke up the porch railings situated between them. From the sidewalk, a narrow concrete walkway made its way through the green grass and to the five steps on the right side of the porch. Balusters on each side of the steps were capped with a handrail painted bright green, the same as the cap running along the porch edge. To the right side of the house, a concrete driveway led to the back of the property and the single car detached garage backed against the rear property line. The driveway was shared with the neighboring house to the right, split only by a wooden fence which divided the two backyards, both of which were completely covered in concrete. For the most part, it looked a lot like all the other houses on the block.

At the top of the stairs leading from the yard to the porch, a single screen door kept the bugs out as the glass-paneled front door lay wide open, allowing the sounds and voices of the party-goers inside to escape the house and spill out onto the neighborhood street. But since all the neighbors had been invited to the Welcome Home party for the Matthews' boy, no one seemed to care.

126

Word had quickly spread around the neighborhood of Ron's accident in Germany and the neighbors were acutely aware of the circumstances of his return and the stress it had put on his parents. Until Ron's awakening three months ago, it was a wait and see game. News of his improvement quickly spread through the neighborhood until "How's Ron doing?" became a daily chant, with neighbors stopping each other on the streets to see who had the latest information.

His return from Walter Reed following two months in recovery after his rather theatrical return to the living, and his thirty day recovery at home had the neighbors abuzz. Initially staying inside, but gradually moving to the front porch and the warm sun, he received the good wishes from his friends and acquaintances in a calm manner, revealing few of the details of his harrowing experience and none of the sorrow he felt for losing his co-pilot.

"Few would understand it," he thought as he graciously acknowledged his new found pedestal.

To celebrate Ron's return both from Germany and the medical experience at Walter Reed, his parents decided to host an open house for their relatives, friends, and neighbors. It was not to be anything elaborate, just some punch and light refreshments, and the chance to share in the joy that was evident in the eyes of Ruth and Paul Matthews. And so they came, bearing small gifts of food and flowers, with an occasional bottle of bootleg whiskey surfacing among the guests. This was a happy time, besides the return of the Matthews' boy, the war had ended on both fronts and many of the soldiers, sailors, and airmen were returning. Imperialism had been halted, though not at a cheap price, and democracy had triumphed. Americans longed to return to the days where America did its thing and other countries did theirs. Few understood that those times were gone, and from now on America's role in the world would be that of leader. But this night was not about that. It was about Ron.

The house was pretty much filled with guests seeking to shake Ron's hand and wish him well. The older men wanted to talk about "their war," recounting the brutal trench warfare they endured during WWI while the women waited for the opportune moment to introduce their daughter or their niece, "you know, the daughter of my husband's brother and his wife from Staten Island. She could not wait to meet you." He smiled, shook their hand, and thanked them for coming such a far distance. He was flattered.

Ron moved easily through the house, giving each guest their fair amount of time before moving on to the next. Moving from the kitchen in the back of the house toward the front living room, he made sure that he made time for everyone. It seemed like it would never end, as some guests left while others arrived. It was like a flowing river of good wishes that never ceased, and while he appreciated it, it eventually got old. But he kept at it, not wanting to embarrass his folks and seem ungrateful.

When it seemed that he was all "hand-shaken" out, Ron found himself just inside the screen door leading to the porch. He quietly slipped out the door, closing it gently, and moved to the far end of the moonlit structure, slowly sinking into a metal rocking chair that creaked as he sat. The noise of the guests inside the house continued, but seemed to lose a considerable amount of its volume, muffled as it were by the night's darkness and the cooler temperature outside.

"This feels good," thought Ron, as he sat there alone.

He could hear the screen door open slightly and sensed, more than saw, a man's head peering outside.

"Ron?" the head said.

"Hi, Dad," Ron answered. "Just getting some air."

"Yea" his Dad said. "Getting a little noisy and crowded in there, but things are beginning to thin out. Have you given any thought to what you are going to do now that the world seems to have calmed down a little? You know, I am getting a little old, and the store is still there for you and I would like to keep it in the family. It has been good to us" he said as if his hard work had nothing to do with its success.

Ron had thought about this moment for a while and had actually dreaded its coming, but here it was.

"Dad," Ron said slowly and somewhat sadly. "I don't think I want to go into the hardware business and work at the store. I love to fly and want to continue doing that. You know the Air Force won't let me back in because of my injuries so I was thinking of buying a surplus C-47 and starting a small cargo service here on the East coast. Nothing like that seems to exist here and it could work. Most cargo movement now is by rail and there are limitations on that, not the least of which is the need for tracks. If you are not located near tracks, you can't use Railway

Express to get your goods. And, at the very least, I'll be able to keep flying."

Ron's father stood silently for a couple of minutes before speaking.

"I would like to see you take over the store. With the tensions around the world easing, business should grow all over, the building industry will start to take off and with all the soldiers returning home, the need for hardware for home improvements long delayed because of the war and the blockade will become a top priority. And after what your mother and I went through with the accident, I don't think we could survive another episode like that. Please think about it, Son, it will be a nice life for you and we would feel a lot better knowing you were on the ground."

Ron seemed to have expected this plea, and with a little wetness forming in his eyes, he reminded his Father of how he had left the old country when his own father, Ron's grandfather, had objected to him moving to America to find his own life.

"So Dad, where does it say that the father can find his own destiny and the son can't?"

The father, pausing for a minute, nods his head in understanding. Ron got up from the chair and embraced his father, like only a son can embrace his father. Looking each other in the eye, both chuckle a little, and walk back to the party.

Chapter Twenty

Ron heard the whine of the plane's engines as it prepared to roll down the runway outside his office window. Over the past twenty-five years, he had heard that sound more often than not. He glanced out the window and saw the silver plane with the Condor insignia streaking down the concrete strip. He had started Condor Airlines shortly after getting out of the hospital and was proud of his company and what he had accomplished. Starting with a single C-47 surplus aircraft, Condor Airlines had grown to over one hundred aircraft of all sizes and capabilities. With that capability, he had brought the economic boom to the smallest of towns scattered throughout the country. It was this capability, the ability to service even the remotest areas of the country that had brought him and his company success. His success was tied to the service of others, a key concept in his business plan and his life.

Ron glanced at the calendar on his desk to check his schedule for the next few days. It was going to be a busy time as the company celebrated its anniversary over the next three days.

"1973," he mumbled to himself. "Where had the years gone? Seems like I just started this business and now it practically runs itself."

He looked around the office, two sides of which were windows overlooking Newark Airport. He could see the constant air traffic landing and taking off, carrying the business of Americans throughout the world.

On one corner of his desk was a simple but elegant framed picture of his wife of twenty years, Lannis. He recalled with a smile her introduction to him the night of his party. "Hi Ron, welcome home," she had said when he entered the living room from the porch. He had turned to say the requisite "thank you, it's good to be home," but never finished it. Instead, he stopped in mid-sentence and starred at the little girl who lived five houses down the street. Only she was not a little girl any more. Three years younger than Ron, she had grown into an attractive, mature woman, graduated college a year ahead of time, and was working as an assistant to a local attorney while attending graduate school. After a two year courtship, they were married in St. Peter's Church in New Brunswick. Life was good.

The other corner of the desk was home to another picture, this time his two children, Melissa, age 12, and Katie, age 10. They were the apples of his eyes, and doted upon as only a successful father could. It was for them that he had built his company, the same way that his father had built the hardware business for his son. He hoped his kids would take and nurture it for their off-spring for generations to come.

Ron had become somewhat of a hero in his community as a result of his success and his sharing nature. He still lived in New Brunswick and drove up the New Jersey turnpike every day to his corner office. But he never forgot where he came from and was constantly helping organizations in need of assistance; be it financially or by allowing his employees to take time to volunteer. He encouraged his employees to help out organizations to the betterment of their communities and this resulted in an employee dedication to Condor which was exemplary, to the dismay of his competitors.

Ron had been approached to run for public office, but had turned down the opportunity. He didn't like the spotlight, and in fact, was kind of shy about his success, giving instead, the credit to others. His one self-indulgence was an old C-47 that he occasionally flew, but for the most part, was parked inside one of Condor's hangers. Shiny and well-cared for, the plane caused new employees to wonder what that was all about, and it pleased the old-timers no end to tell the story of the plane and the founder of the company.

Ron's thoughts turned to the next day, the 25th Anniversary party of Condor Airlines. He had carefully scheduled the extravaganza to ensure that all his employees would be able to attend. He set it up in a huge hanger away from most of the usual noise of an airport. He had actually closed the company down for three days, notifying his customers well in advance, so that all the employees could be there. Those employees, and there were many, who lived outside the local area were either flown or provided train transportation to the Newark area. He put them up in several of the better hotels in the area, picking up the tab for all the expenses. He reasoned that his success was due to their hard work and that they and their families should share in the celebration.

He looked around the office with a sense of pride, packed up his briefcase, flicked off the overhead light and walked out of his office. He passed Margaret, his loyal secretary of fifteen years, and headed toward the door.

Stopping at the door, he turned and said to Margaret, "Margaret, get out of here and go home. We have a big day tomorrow and I want to see your smiling face having a good time."

Margaret lifted her head up from a stack of papers. "Good night, Ron," she said with a knowing smile on her face.

Chapter Twenty-One

The huge hanger looked more like a movie set then a maintenance facility. Balloons and streamers hung from the rafters, signs of congratulations adorned the stark walls, many from competitors acknowledging the success of Condor Airlines. In truth, the outside metal walls hid the temporary fantasyland that astounded the adults and brought squeals of delight to the youngsters. Though far away from most of the air traffic, the roar of the engines from planes departing the airport could still be heard as they screamed down the runway, heading south along the Jersey coast until they turned toward their final destination.

But the Condor airplanes were still, standing as a tribute to those employees who ran them. Having closed the airline down for three days, Ron had invited his employees to the celebration. Those who lived out of town were provided transportation to Newark, either by air or train, and put up in the better hotels near the airport so they could also participate in the festivities. All expenses were charged to the company.

Inside the party hanger, several airplanes, all with the Condor markings were placed around the large open space. Kids of all ages, many of them seeing airplanes up close for the first time, scrambled over, around, and in each of them, moving from one pilot's seat to the next as they imagined themselves in command of the metal monsters. The kids all wore pilot's hats, appropriately sized for smaller heads, they had been given upon entry to the hanger. The employees would each receive something more substantial, but that would be reserved till later when each found an extra check in their pay envelope. Ron was not one to not take care of his own. He had been fortunate and wanted to share that fortune with them.

A podium stood in front of the airplanes, a large projection screen hanging above and behind the podium. During the festivities, pictures of different people were flashed on the screen and the kids squealed with delight when their father or mother suddenly took the spotlight. Mathews moved around the hanger, visiting with the out-of-state folks, meeting their wives and kids and just enjoying himself. He stopped and talked with anyone willing to speak to him, especially those who had help him build the company.

There was Dick Russell, a boyhood friend who knew nothing about aviation, but all there was to know about operating a business. He left the technical stuff to Mathews. His forte was dollars, how to get them, how to use them to make more, and what to do with the more. Matthews was Mr. Outside, dealing with the power brokers and sharks who constantly threatened to run away with the airline, while Russell was Mr. Inside and ran the day to day operations of the company.

There was Jack Ross, an operations wizard who practically invented the next-day delivery. He worked for Russell, but in reality, they trusted each other's ability to the extent they were more like peers.

136

Then there was Margaret Vargas, a long time resident of New Brunswick. She grew up there, married, had grown kids who eventually moved away, been widowed, and worked now because she liked the way Condor gave back to the community. The company had denoted a considerable amount of money to St. Peter's Hospital when her husband died there of cancer, all in her husband's name. Nobody knew this but Margaret, Dick, and of course Matthews. Margaret was the Executive Secretary and everyone knew she spoke for Matthews. She had been with him for fifteen years and knew, even before he did, what decisions he would make on all but a few topics. Those she didn't, she quietly waited for, then made sure they were implemented at once and without delay. She was a confidant and a friend and someone Matthews could trust.

Dick Russell moved to the platform, introduces himself, and starts to speak.

"Hello, everyone, and welcome to twenty-five years of instant success! We are all here because of the vision, the hard work, and the successful embodiment of that vision in my company, your company, our company, Condor Airlines. Started as a one-plane operation, it gradually expanded to be part of this country's aviation industry, founded on the principles of honestly, hard work, and the company family, a family who puts the customer first in all its doings. We can be proud of what we do, and how we do it, and we can be proud of the one man who started the company and shared his vision with all of us. Ladies and gentlemen, please allow me to introduce Mr. Ron Matthews!"

Matthews bounded up the stairs to the platform and raised his hands like a fighter after a victory, and with a big smile on his face, acknowledges the cheers and applause from his employees and their families. He looks around at the crowd and walks to the microphone as the crowd noise begins to wane.

"I want to thank all of you from coming here today, taking time from your busy lives to join us in celebrating this momentous day. All of us in some way or another are responsible for the success we celebrate today. I would like to acknowledge the tremendous work and effort some individuals who may not be well known within the company, but without whose professional efforts we would not be as successful as we are. First, there is Bill Snyder, Head of Maintenance. Without his experience and expertise we would be a storage company and not an airline." The crowd laughed and applauded.

"Then there is our Head of Personnel, Janet Dickson, whom we have all met and who helps making sure we have the best people working for us. And of course, who could ever over look our Head of Security, Richard Means, whose tireless efforts and oversight ensure our safety and the safety of those we serve."

"But there are others. For instance, there is Richard Alveraz, a shipping clerk in the Phoenix office, Mattie McDonald, one of our customer service representatives in Denver, and even Don Woods, a maintenance engineer in the New York office. These are the people who come face-to-face with the customer, and if they don't satisfy them, we all lose. And to them we owe a debt of gratitude."

138

A resounding applause and thank yous broke out among the rapt crowd.

"And there is Margaret, who is the only one who really knows what is going on" says Matthews with a big smile as Margaret's face flashes up on the screen wearing a crown on her head and carrying a baseball bat in her hands. A large cheer erupts at the caricature on the screen.

Ron continues to talk and makes one final tribute to his parents. They scolded him when he needed it, supported when he didn't know he needed it, and taught him the attributes that are now the backbone of the company.

Suddenly, Margaret appeared on the podium, moving over to Ron. She acknowledges the cheers her appearance raised and whispered something in Ron's ear.

"Ron, recommend you wrap it up as people are getting restless, not to mention hungry. Besides, you have an important phone call waiting."

He nodded in acceptance, moved one last time to the microphone, thanking everyone for the work and their attendance at the party. Waving he walked away.

Margaret stepped to the mike saying, "Well, we got through that part, now let's get this party started."

The band began to play a lively tune as the waiters brought trays and trays of food to the tables and the festivities began.

Chapter Twenty-Two

When Ron walked into the company headquarters on Monday morning, the offices were alive with everyone talking about the party over the weekend. Peals of laughter came from folks recounting the good times they had with their families, their kids, and their co-workers, many of whom they met in person for the first time. Ron acknowledged the waves and smiles and quickly moved passed Margaret, who sat there with her own little grin and into his office. His closed door quickly reopened and he said to Margaret to come to him in about ten minutes to set something up. Just as quickly, the door closed and she could hear him start talking on the phone.

With a soft knock on the door, Margaret came into Ron's office as instructed, pen and pad in hand ready to take notes. "Margaret," Ron said. "Please call a regular staff meeting for nine-thirty this morning and add about five more chairs to the conference room as there are others that I have invited to attend. Also please make yourself available as well as there will be follow-up actions which need to be documented and distributed. Oh, and thank you for all the work you did for the party. It was amazing and it seems as though everyone had a great time. And your efforts are appreciated. Thank you. OK, see you at nine-thirty." With that, he turned his attention back to some papers on his desk he had been reading.

Ron could hear some whispering voices through the door between his office and the conference room, glanced down at his watch, confirmed the time with his desk clock and started gathering multiple papers from his strewn desk, arranging them in some type of order that only he could understand. He got up, walked across the open space between his desk and the conference room door, took a deep breath, and walked into the room where about 20 people stood, waiting for the meeting to begin. At exactly nine-thirty, Margaret came through the main door of the room and moved to her normal seat. With that, Ron asked everyone to be seated and sat down in his usual seat at the end of the conference table. All was silent.

"Good morning," Ron said, as he surveyed the others in the room. "Today we have a unique opportunity before us and we have to decide not whether to take it, but rather how to take it. Saturday evening, after being so graciously ushered off the stage by Margaret, I had a phone call waiting for me. It was not a regular phone call, but a call that could determine the future course of Condor Airlines. It came from a company in the Midwest, a company we and millions of others know and follow. A company well known for its unique way of doing business. A company which mirrors ours in the way they treat their customers and the service they provide. The company is Gateway Computers.

A murmur erupted in the room. With all the attendees being in the business world, they had read about Gateway or had successful business dealings

141

with them, and knew them to be a shining light in the business community, run by a group of business professionals who were dedicated to serving those in need of their products and services. A standard to which other companies strove to achieve.

"Their senior management," Ron continued, "has decided to take the company to new heights, offering its customers the fastest possible delivery, even one day at times, in an attempt to obviously attract more business, but to also be the first to offer such a service. And they want Condor to be part of it.

After looking at several options and several different companies, their management has chosen Condor to be the sole transportation provider in meeting this new service. They have requested that we assemble and provide them a comprehensive plan to do just that. We would pick up the packages at their manufacturing facilities and transport them to the front door of the customer. They will provide us their plans, along with a Non--Disclosure Agreement which everyone in this room will be required to sign, and we will use their plans around which to build ours."

"This is a huge undertaking as it will require probably new hubs, new distribution facilities, new vehicles designed to deliver door-to-door packages, and of course, additional personnel. New and different planes will probably be needed also. It will be our biggest effort yet, and if done with the planning and accuracy with which Condor is known, will result in us being the leading company we all want us to be. The opportunity is now, and the decision is ours."

"I throw in one word of discouragement. They want our proposal in three weeks time."

142

Chapter Twenty-Three

The silence in the room was deafening. Attendees waited, hoping that this was a joke. As that possibility waned, one strong voice broke the silence.

"Ron," said Dick. "That's an almost impossible task given the day to day operations we have going on. All of us here, and those who are not here, are working hard on our regular jobs. I don't know how we can afford to take time from those to work this proposal at all, least of all in three weeks. I think the opportunity is a great one but to put together a proposal we all can be proud of, and more importantly to be able to act upon and put the proposal into action, it is going to take more than three weeks, more like three months or even more. Why is there such a hurry on their part?"

"When I spoke with their President," Ron explained, "He said that they had just made the decision to adopt the new strategy but to do that they needed increased capital funding. To get that funding required the issuance of new bonds, which in turn required the approval of their Board of Governors. The next Board of Governors meeting is scheduled four weeks from now, or one week after our proposal is due. If they missed that meeting it will mean waiting another year before the next one, unless a special meeting is requested. And special meetings are rarely approved."

"So," Ron continued, "It's now or sometime next year. And their desire for now is fueled by the fear that someone else will be the first one to offer this service, leaving Gateway in the dust. And, like we usually say, "If you're not leading the pack, the view is always the same." And, again like us, they don't like that view."

Ron continued to explain the rudiments of his discussion with Gateway. The Condor proposal would be an important part of the Gateway presentation to their Board as it would explain how the delivery service would work, how different parts of the country would be serviced, how Condor would tailor its facilities, its flights and its home deliveries to mesh with what Gateway would offer its customers. Equally important the proposal would explain the financial commitment Condor would be making to ensure the success of the new strategy. It would analyze the requirements and itemize the costs associated with those requirements. It would outline the operational aspects of the strategy and make sure it furthers that strategy rather than get in the way of it.

"Why would different parts of the country be serviced any differently than the others?" asked one of the Regional Directors.

The reason, Ron explained, had to do with the Region's make up and the geographic conditions within it. For example, he continued, compare a Region containing New York City with a mid-west Region. New York City itself is an old city, with lots of buildings, lots of people, and little empty space. Deliveries to business usually take place in small alleys with doors to the business in the alleys or

144

behind the store. In the mid-west there is a lot of more space between the stores and deliveries can be made either via back streets or even through front doors. There are also malls which house many stores with easy delivery locations. Homes are usually grouped together but not on top of one-another making home delivery easier. Now, think of the trucks that would have to make deliveries in both of the Regions. In the mid-west, trucks can be large, carry lots of product for delivery and can handle a day's worth of deliveries in one load. In New York City, things are different. With small alleys, delivery trucks have to be small to fit in those alleys. Deliveries cannot be made on the main streets because of the blockage of traffic. And with smaller trucks, the capacity is smaller requiring either more vehicles per day or multiple trips per vehicle. That is only one example of the differences that need to be analyzed, addressed, and resolved.

Ron could see some nodding of heads as the picture became clearer. "This is not a democracy," he said. "So we will not have a vote on proceeding or not. However, I do value the opinion of all of you and invite your thoughts on any aspect of the subject. After hearing them, I will make the decision as to proceed or not. Margaret, please takes notes on what points are raised so I can review them."

"Now, the floor is open. Please educate me."

The discussion began slowly. Actually it was more questions than comments. Some of them were answered when information from Gateway was brought to the conference room. Those answered were scratched off of Margaret's list while the remaining ones were left to be settled at a later date. As time went on the comments turned from "if we can meet that requirement" to "how can we meet that requirement." This subtle difference pleased Ron as he had pretty much decided they were going to do it. Now his team was looking at how to get it done rather than offering excuses as to why it could not be done.

Lunch was ordered and delivered as the discussion continued. By early afternoon assignments were being distributed to those in the room with the Regional Directors being responsible for their Regions input as to assets needed to fulfill their obligations as well as to the policies and procedures for their usage. The Regional input would be consolidated by the corporate staff, reviewed by a proposal Red Team and finally submitted to Gateway by the requested due date.

Finally Ron stood up. "Well," he said. "We seem to have reached the conclusion that this is something we should do and have pretty much outlined a plan as to how to do it. And we can do this. If, during your preparation, something is missing or you need help, don't hesitate to ask. We have enough talent around this table that can help solve any problem. If there are no more questions, let's get started.

Everyone in the room began to stand up, talking excitedly to their neighbor or heading out the door to find a quiet place to call back to their own office.

"Ron," said Margaret. "I am going to need some help in preparing this proposal. Can I bring someone in for the duration?"

"Yes" came the absent-minded response.

Chapter Twenty-Four

The rest of Monday and all day Tuesday were a blur. Between numerous meetings, discussions, phone calls with Condor people as well as Gateway executives asking for clarifications, Williams' work just never seemed finished. Even extending his workday to nine or ten in the evening did not give him the time he needed to satisfactorily work the proposal. He had even slept in the office Tuesday night, something that he considered doing until the effort was completed in a couple of weeks. He knew his kids would miss him, his wife not so much. While the facade they presented to the outside world was one of a loving husband and wife that was no longer the reality of the private life. In fact, their physical interaction had ceased to exist, especially when he had moved into one of the other bedrooms citing his snoring as the reason for his move to the kids. His wife made no objection and did not seem to care. In fact, they had openly discussed the possibility of a divorce and the separation of assets. That was not difficult as long as the kids were comfortable. The kids provided her with what she needed.

Early Wednesday morning, Ron rolled off his office couch, took a quick hot shower, dressed and drove over to the all-night diner near the airport's administration building The piping hot black coffee and danish helped him wake up as he tried to read the morning paper through his partially closed eyes. The world news was anything but calming, the local news centered on the previous day's shootings, and even his favorite sports teams added to the negativity. Only the comics showed any kind of positivity, so he read them slowly, sometimes more than once, and allowed himself to enjoy them.

After an hour, he drove back to the headquarters and walked to his office. Margaret was there already, handling some minor crisis and waved as he walked past her. Near Margaret's area were two visiting executive cubicles completely provided with all the latest office equipment and supplies so that visiting Condor executives could continue their duties while at the corporate office. Matthews noticed that one was occupied by a young woman. She is about twenty-four, maybe twenty-five, slender in build, short blonde hair that barely reached her shoulders. She appeared busy at whatever tasks she was doing, but looked up at Matthews, smiled and nods. He returns the nod without saying a word, looks to Margaret and motions her to join him in his office. She nods, holds one finger up to ask for a couple of minutes, and returns to finish the call. He nodded in understanding and entered his office.

Two quiet knocks on the office door signified that Margaret was about to enter, and enter she did, waving papers, a big smile on her face, and grinning from ear to ear. She started to read the papers, some just little notes on hotel stationary, some more formal, but all of them thanking Ron for the wonderful way he had shown his employees his appreciation of them and also their family. The kids had loved the planes, the games they played had everyone involved, the food was plentiful and good, and the atmosphere just super. They appreciated the hotels and transportation and a lot of them said they would never work for another company again. Ron smiled as the notes were read and he began to realize a little, not much but a little, how his small gesture meant to those who worked for him. He vowed to do more of it.

Holding his hand up to stop the incessant chattering of Margaret, Ron asked "who is the young woman sitting out by you?"

"Don't you remember, when we discussed the proposal to Gateway I said that I would need some help in assembling the document and I asked if I could bring someone on to help me. You said yes, I could. Looking through many resumes personnel had, she seemed like a good candidate. She has a BA degree in business and had done some intern work with Johnson and Johnson, which was a good recommendation right there. I called her the next morning, had an interview that afternoon, and she started work here this morning. Is there something wrong with that?"

"No Margaret, there is nothing wrong with that. I had just forgotten about that conversation till you reminded me. I definitely trust your judgment, so let's just move on. She works for you. Keep her busy and remember who we are and how we do things. Now, let's go over a few things I noticed in one of the write ups. Oh, by the way, since she is going to be working with us, at least tell me her name."

"Natalie," Margaret replied.

"Natalie," Ron thought. "Nice name"

"Now look at this write-up from this Region," he started. "They have pretty much covered all the elements that we had discussed, you know, personnel, equipment, warehouse space, vehicles, but they have done it in a superficial manner. For instance they say *'We will use fifteen new trucks to ensure the fastest delivery.'* That is all well and good, but what size of trucks since that Region has both rural and urban space. Do they need ten large ones and five small ones, or vice versa. And with more trucks, there is a need for more drivers. And something which almost every Regions forgets is that with more vehicles, there is a need for more mechanics. A vehicles does no good if it sits for days waiting for it to be fixed before resuming its intended purpose."

"We have to think like the Gateway board members will be thinking. They are being asked to provide more money for their operation and want to be sure of what they are getting. If we don't tell them up front, they will start to ask questions and we have little time to provide answers to them. We have to beat them to the punch to prevent that from happening. We need to communicate these concerns to all the Regions.

"Margaret" thought Ron, "have Natalie put together a list of questions that she believes the Gateway Board members will be asking. I think she has the education and experience with Johnson and Johnson to be able to do so. If not, we shall soon know. Schedule a meeting with the three of us this afternoon to go over the questions, add or subtract as needed and we can send it out to use in formulating out response."

"Well," thought Ron as Margaret turned and left. "She has the beauty, let's see if she has the brains."

150

Chapter Twenty-Five

The rest of the morning was pretty much like the last one, meetings, phone calls, discussions, disagreements, resolutions, and most of all, progress. Initial write-ups were beginning to pour in from the Regions to be reviewed first by the respective corporate department then to Dick, and finally to Ron. All the recommended changes were added or subtracted from the submissions by either Margaret or Natalie and the progress was noted on the status boards.

Status boards were positioned round the conference room, one for each of the Condor Regions. Each board identified elements with which the Region had to be concerned and under each element were sub-elements or sub-topics relating to each element. Round sticky tabs were used to quickly identify the status of the sub-elements, red meaning it was being worked, yellow meaning it was under review, and green meaning the sub-element was complete. Only when all the sub-elements were "green" could the element itself be considered "green" and only when all the elements were classified "green" would the Region be considered "green" and its input to the final proposal ready to be integrated with the rest. This morning the status boards showed mostly red with a couple of yellows. There were no greens on the boards indicating that there was still a lot of work to be done.

Ron walked into the conference room and listened as Margaret explained to Natalie the purpose of the boards and how to update them. Ron and Margaret had used this system before and were comfortable with it and it allowed a person to instantly see the status of any particular element or sub -element giving the corporate departments Directors an idea of which Regions may be in need of help or just a kick in the butt."

"Lots of reds, Margaret," Ron said. "How often are you updating the boards?"

"I try to update them as the changes happen, but the changes happen so often I'd spend most of my day walking back and forth from my desk to here so I've set up sort of a schedule of ten am, noon, three pm and when I leave. Natalie and I have worked out a system where I come in the regular time and leave the regular time and she comes in around noon and leaves when you are done. That way you have coverage the whole time you are working," Margaret explained, "and I don't burn out."

Ron looked at Natalie and asked, "You ok with that?"

Natalie nodded in concurrence and said, "I only live a couple of miles from here and since I have a car, transportation is not a problem. I can get my things done in the morning and easily be here by noon. Driving home later in the evening is easy also since most of the traffic is gone and the roads are well lit. I'm good with the arrangement."

And so the next couple of days followed that routine. On Friday afternoon, Ron called both

Margaret and Natalie into his office for a quick conference.

Ron started the conversation by talking about the upcoming weekend. "Tomorrow is Saturday," he said, "and I expect anyone associated with the preparation of this proposal to be working. They, of course, will be compensated accordingly. And I want lunch brought in so there is less stoppage in effort during lunch hour. However," he continued, "I want no one working on Sunday other than those routinely scheduled for Sunday. That means this office is closed on Sunday. I consider Sunday to be a family day and I want my employees to enjoy that day with their families."

"Margaret, please send a memo out to all employees thanking them for the efforts they are putting forth on this and include my guidance as to this week-end work. Natalie, this guidance includes you. I want you to spend some time with your family also."

Natalie nodded as Margaret glanced over at her. "I am sure the people will appreciate the gesture about Sunday, she said," but I have no one here to share the day with. My family, what is left of them, live in the Chicago area and while we talk often, the actual visits are far and few between."

"I thought you were local?" asked Ron with a quizzical look on his face.

"Well, I did go to school locally, Douglas College in New Brunswick. I was awarded a scholarship and decided to take the opportunity to study business there with the possibility of a follow-on job in the New York area. The internship with Johnson and

Johnson was a real eye-opener for me and when that ended, and this position came open, I jumped at the chance to learn more. It has been a good experience for me. Margaret has taught me a lot and seeing how you run the company as a family gives me fresh ideas as to the role of senior management. It has been good."

"Margaret," Ron said nodding appreciatively, "we may have to keep this one. Get with HR in the next couple of days and see what we have available. I don't want to lose her."

Margaret smiled, grabbed Natalie by the arm as they scrambled out the door chatting like old friends. Ron watched them go, smiled and nodded to himself.

Meanwhile, Natalie's memo containing questions the Gateway board might ask and which should be answered in the proposal prior to them being asked caused a turmoil in the company. Previously, questions raised by a proposal were answered in a volley-like manner. Asked, answered. Asked, answered. Asked, answered. But this time, all the answers had to be in the initial proposal. Pages were pulled, sections completely rewritten, assumptions replaced with researched answers and any doubts that Condor knew what was required were quickly, quietly, and efficiently wiped away. The proposal was becoming a solid foundation upon which to prove Condor's value as a reliable partner. Ron was satisfied with the effort and the resultant work.

Chapter Twenty-Six

Saturday seemed like any other work day. People came and went as they usually do. Margaret was there when Ron woke up and had his coffee ready. The write-ups were coming in fast and furious as the first week of preparation was drawing to a close. Some tense moments were showing their ugly face as the writers, managers, department heads and even Dick and Ron tried to convince others how points should be made, or not made, and what reasonable costs should be associated with their points. Natalie's questions, as Ron had begun to refer to them, was causing much more work, but resulted in Regions evaluating their own submissions through the eyes of the Gateway board. It was strenuous and detailed work and by the time that Natalie walked into the office, Margaret was swamped with revisions that practically covered her whole desk.

"Thank goodness you are here" said Margaret, I was beginning to get over-whelmed. Have you had lunch, there is some in the small conference room?"

"I had a late breakfast so I'm ok for now," said Natalie. "Where do you want me to start?"

"Start with this stack. Try to work all the revisions from the same Region. I'm trying to put some order into this process, and quite honestly, it's not working. People are putting their comments on one pile without regard to where it should go and I have to search the whole pile each time to stay on the same page. We have never had such a big proposal like this before and it's a little daunting."

Natalie smiled and left the room, returning in a couple of minutes with a couple of maintenance men carrying a big table. They set the table up against the wall between Margaret's and Natalie's desks as Natalie moved to her desk and began to make signs of stiff paper, one sign for each Region. Placing them on the table she turned to Margaret and told her that each paper represented a Region and when someone came to drop off a revision, they should place it in the right Region. That way, Regions revisions can be controlled and followed. Margaret liked the idea and started using it right away. It proved effective as a more organized information flow made the work easier.

Ron was constantly moving, checking the status boards frequently, checking with Margaret and Natalie to see how they were holding up under the rush. Both seemed to be doing well and Natalie's work-flow fix made the review and revision process more controlled. Between the checking, he was reading the inputs, making suggestions, calling into question why changes were needed or not needed. It was a busy day.

Margaret knocked softly on the door, walked in and told Ron that it was five o'clock and she was leaving and would see him on Monday. "Natalie is still here," she said and would take care of whatever he needed. Ron smiled and nodded in appreciation of her efforts that day and said "Have a quiet evening and a restful Sunday, we have another busy week ahead of us."

With that she turned and quickly walked out of the office to head home.

Ron worked diligently without looking at the clock. Natalie would come into the office periodically to bring in new updates and pick up the reviewed ones for incorporation into the proposed final document or to return them to the Regions for their review and approval. During one such visit she reached to deposit reviews into Ron's in-box as he absentmindedly reached for the next one and for the first time their hands touched. Natalie quickly spoke up and said, "I'm sorry." They both looked down at the touching hands, neither in any hurry to move them. "No problem," Ron said. "Your hands are nice and soft."

"Thank you," she said, slowly withdrawing her hand. "Well back to work. There is a lot to do." She turned headed back to her desk..\ Barely out of Ron's office, she raised the touched hand and gave it a little kiss and resumed the trek to her desk. Soon she was hard at work doing what she was hired to do.

Ron watched her walk away, her hips causing the loose skirt to sway and her heels clicking as they touched the floor. She exited the office and returned to her desk. He returned to his task at hand, his mind in a completely other place.

And so it begins.

He remembered that afternoon when he met his now wife, Lannis. He remembered her standing there just to say hello and welcome home. He remembered the glow in her eyes, the softness of her hand as he took it, and the smile on her face as he suggested meeting sometime in the future away from the crowd.

He remembered the joy of their wedding, the thrill of the honeymoon, and the happiness of knowing their first child was soon to be. And the magnification of that happiness upon hearing the news of the second child.

And he also remembered the strange and somewhat unknowing erosion of that happiness slowly drifting away. Why, he had asked himself many times, but he came up with no solid answer. And while he thrashed about in the uncertainty, he could sense his wife going through the same conflict. Soon there was little communication other than that about the children and their schoolwork. Lannis would spend her time with her friends, leaving Ron alone at night, which prompted the building of the office bedroom. As time went by, he used it more than the house. And soon, they were living an empty existence, fueled and kept together only by the two kids they both loved.

Chapter Twenty-Seven

A couple of hours later he released his mind from the papers on his desk and looked around the office. He got up and walked around his desk to the outer office and saw Natalie still hard at work there. He walked over to her desk and stopped in front of it.

"I think it's about time to call it a day," he said. She looked up at him. "Why don't you give it a rest and go home and---, wait," he continued. "I know of a little place around the corner that serves real good pizza. If you have no other plans, perhaps you would like to join me and we can relax together?"

Natalie thought for a quick minute. "That sounds like a plan to me. I have no other plans and a slice or two of pizza sounds appetizing."

"OK," he said. "Let's wrap things up around here and I'll meet you by the front door."

Ten minutes later they met by the front door. Ron activated the security system, held the door for Natalie, and locked it behind her. "Let's drive in my car. I know the way and since I will be coming back here tonight, you can pick up your car after we eat."

She looked at him with a questioning look on her face. "Why are you coming back here?" she asked.

After a pregnant pause Ron said, "It's a long story. We can talk about it over pizza."

Ten minutes later they pulled into the parking lot and five minutes later were seated at a booth near the back of the tiny restaurant. They ordered drinks and agreed on a pizza and settled in to wait for its delivery to their table.

"Well," said Natalie, "what's the long story?"

He stared intently into her eyes and tried to remember the last ten years and how best to explain it, something he had never done before. "About ten years ago," he started, "my wife and I started to grow apart. I don't know why or even how that happened, but it did. It was after the birth of our second child and it seemed like the magic was gone. Oh we were cordial and polite to each other but the spark that drove us together in the first place seemed to have extinguished itself. Her interests were centered around the kids, which was a good thing. My interests became centered around the growth of the company which was a not so good of a thing. I justified it as being responsible for the well-being of my family and for the families of those working for me and anything less would be irresponsible. I kept plugging away and she kept taking care of the kids, taking them to band practice, soccer games, school activities, all of which I missed because of work. This continued on for years and she was getting frustrated at me because of it. Our intimate moments became far and few between and it became apparent that our togetherness as a family was being split. After years of trying to figure out what was happening and even going to some counseling, she asked me if I wanted a divorce. I said no. I was not going to admit to failure so I decided, we decided, to stay together to ensure that the kids were cared for. Even now that sounds stupid as I had not been there for them for years. But that was the

160

reasoning we used for ourselves. In reality, it may have been the desire to maintain our social standing, our friends, or whatever. In any event, we stayed together. After that discussion, I told my wife that I was moving into the spare room so as to not have her feel that she had to be intimate with me. We have not had sex since that evening. When the new building was being built, I had a small room added to my office with a closet, bathroom, and small bed that I could use on those nights when I worked late and did not want to go home. It was just sometimes easier than trying to deal with the reality of the situation. Last week we discussed and agreed on arrangements for a divorce. It is interesting how discussions with a wife swiftly turn to negotiations when a divorce raises its ugly head. We decided to keep it quiet until it is completed. That should be in a couple of weeks as we know some people who can push it through. After that, there is no more hiding it."

Ron paused, and paused some more. It was the first time that he had tried to verbally explain to anyone what had been and was happening at home. He was not even sure that he had explained it correctly, just that is how he recalled it at the time.

He leaned back in his chair, let out a painful sigh and stared at Natalie, trying to guess what her reaction would be.

Natalie had leaned forward while Ron was talking, listening to every word and trying to understand both the words and the meaning behind them. When he was done, she reached across the table and gently rested her hand on his. "I'm sorry," she said. "I should not have been so intrusive."

161

"No sorry needed. I needed to hear it myself."

The pizza came and their conversation turned to other things which continued during the ride back to the office. Ron parked next to Natalie's car and walked her to the door. She got in and rolled the window down to say good night. Ron bent down to give her a kiss. With a pixie-like smile, she raised her hand and with one finger turned his head sideways. With that, she leaned forward and gave him a soft kiss on his cheek.

"Later," she said, put the car in gear and drove off. Ron watched as she drove away, smiled and went to his office and to bed remembering that word "later".

Natalie walked into her apartment, sat down, picked up the phone and dialed a number. An older woman answered on the other end. "Momma," said Natalie, "I think I found the one," began the two hour conversation.

Chapter Twenty-Eight

"Why," said the elderly voice. The word resounded through Natalie's brain as if it were a gunshot.

"Why" is a funny word," she thought. It is small, only three little letters, two close together in the alphabet both divided and joined by a third which lies somewhere near the beginning. But it is a strong word, causing people to think, to reason, and to articulate a purpose for doing something. It causes one to dig into the mind, not with a shovel or even a big heavy machine scratching the mere surface. It is more like a huge boulder crashing its way through the emotional ocean till it reaches the bedrock of thought, revealing the truth. She was not there yet.

"Momma," she said," you taught me to judge people not only by the things they do and how they do them, but also what they don't do, and how they don't do them. I have only known this gentleman for a week, and I don't use that term "gentleman" lightly. I have seen him work around people, seen him interact with employees from vice presidents to maintenance personnel, to janitors. He treats them all the same, respecting them for the jobs they are doing, praising them for the work they are doing and encouraging them to extend themselves and be the best they can be. On the other hand, I have seen him quietly take an employee aside and counsel him as to how to do better, not in front of others, but rather one on one. And I have seen employees after such a session return with tears in their eyes for having failed this man, and redouble their efforts to do better. People don't do that for others who don't care for them."

"This man is smart and confident," she continued, "and believes he can make a difference, not only in the business world, but also in the lives of those who work with him. I told you before that my position is a temporary one, helping put together a proposal which would be a big step in the growth of the company. The primary admin and I have worked out a schedule where she comes to work in the morning and leaves around five o'clock in the evening. I come in around noon and stay until the day is done, usually around nine in the evening. It works well, and since most of the employees leave around five or six, I have several hours working directly with this man. During those hours he is usually on the phone with people out west, offering suggestions for improvement, congratulating them on their successes, asking about their families, and generally checking on them. That is something he does not have to do, but he does it."

"Earlier this evening, when things had quieted down, he asked me if I wanted to go for some pizza before we closed for the day. He drove to this little place a couple of miles away and we ordered pizza and a pitcher of coke. We chatted for a while before returning to the office, where he was staying that night. When I questioned him about that, he openly told me that he and his wife were and had been going through a bad time but had decided to stay together for the sake of the children. That time had passed and they had filed for a divorce. He had moved into the spare bedroom, but spent most of his nights at the office, which included a small apartment-like space. After that discussion, I drove home alone and we are talking now."

"As for what he doesn't do, I am at a little bit of a loss because of the short length of time I have known him. I know he doesn't drink, at least he didn't when we had pizza. I know he doesn't smoke as there is not even an ashtray in his office. He doesn't swear, well, not much anyway, and only very quietly when alone. I have not seen or heard him belittle anyone, though it has only been a week, but others I talk with seem to confirm that. Even when someone goes into his office with a question, the answer of which he already knows, he doesn't preach to them when they should know. He uses the Socratic method of teaching by asking questions of the person in such a manner that the person figures out the answer themselves without being told. The result is that both the knowledge and confidence of the person in need comes out of the meeting feeling that they have solved the problem and just needed a little direction and prodding. As a result they will never be afraid to ask for help again. And that is a good thing."

The elderly voice cautioned Natalie to go slowly, take the time to get to know each other in different situations.

"Time reveals many things, both good and bad and while you can't get it back, it is best to use it wisely to help make better decisions. So, no rushing my Dear. Take it slowly as this is something that has many facets, not the least of which is his marriage. Let things sort themselves out and if it is meant to be, it will be. I have known both sides of that and experienced both the joy and the sadness of them. It is part of life. Now, my Dear, it is late here and I need to get some rest. We can talk more tomorrow after you have had a little time to think about it. So, sleep tight my Dear. Love you."

"Good night, Momma. Love you too."

Chapter Twenty-Nine

Ron woke around seven with two things on his mind, "later" and "proposal". But it was soon the latter which came to the front. After getting dressed, he walked directly into the conference room and studied the status boards. Margaret was busy updated the boards with the latest from the week-end. He happily noticed that most of the reds had vanished, replaced with yellows and some greens. One region was done, all its parts covered with green stickers and a smiley green face stared out from the region header. It was a good start for the second week of proposal preparation.

Margaret looked at him and said, "Looks good. We should be wrapping more of the regions up this week. After that will be the actual assembling of the package and the delivery. How do you plan on having it delivered?"

Ron thought for a minute. "We will make three sets of the package," he replied. One will be hand-carried to them on one of our planes. A second will be hand-carried on a commercial flight, and the third will remain here, so we can refer to it if there are any comments or concerns from the other side. That way we should be covered. I'll have Dick pick the people to hand-carry the proposals and set up the flights. You continue to do what you are doing now and remember to use Natalie when you need her. Oh, and thanks for the job you are doing, Margaret. We all appreciate it."

Margaret smiled at the compliment, nodded her head, and turned back to her task.

With that, Ron turned and walked back to his desk. "Later" surged to the front.

The week moved ahead like a roller-coaster, some ups and some downs, but always on the move. Each day started with a quick review of the prior day's results and the determining of the current day's goals. A break was taken when lunch arrived. Ron was successful in sitting near Natalie a couple of times but caution dictated that nobody realize the interaction between the two. As a result, other than eye contact, there was little communication between them.

As Friday rolled around and people began to make plans for the week-end, believing that there would be no work on Saturday or Sunday, Ron took a late lunch after most of the others were done. He sat next to Margaret and they chatted about things other than work. Things like the new buildings that Rutgers was building on the river. They talked about the old neighborhood and what had become of the hardware store. They laughed and shared stories about the old Italian and Hungarian restaurants that used to reside in the area and the corner bars where the old men would spend their afternoons before heading back up the street for their daily nap. They talked about the local Catholic Church where the Mass was said in Latin and the sermon in Hungarian. No one under the age of twenty understood a word the priests were saying. But that was all right as there was nobody at the Mass that was under twenty.

As they were chatting, Natalie walked by the conference room and Margaret motioned her to join them. She said something about work, but Margaret would not take no for an answer and insisted she join them. So she did. The three of them enjoyed the banter that ensued for the next fifteen minutes, until Margaret got a call she had to answer, leaving Ron and Natalie there alone.

"Got any plans for the weekend?" Ron asked.

"The usual stuff one does on free days," Natalie laughingly responded. "Washing, cleaning, shopping, etc. Oh, and I am tinkering with going for my Masters and will possibly visit schools in the area that could offer me what I'm interested in."

Realizing the incorrect syntax in her last sentence she giggled and continued "it probably should be English but that's not my cup of tea. Most likely it will be an MBA with some concentration in a particular business area, like finance or quality. I think both are important and there should be opportunities in either of those fields."

Ron looked quietly at her. "Have you thought about staying here while you go to school. We could use someone like you and we do have an education program that could help pay for some, if not all, of your school expenses?"

Natalie stood up, saying "I would like that if possible. Now, I have to go back to work before the boss gets upset with my incessant chatter." She turned to leave the conference room and go to her desk.

"One more thing before you go," Ron said. "Would you like some pizza again this evening. I know this little place around the corner," he asked, with a sly grin on his face.

169

"I wondered if you would ask again," she replied, with an equally sly grin. Turning to leave, she seemed to float back to her desk, anticipating another good pizza and pleasant company. "A great way to start the week-end," she thought.

Chapter Thirty

What was anticipated to be a quick pizza soon expanded to last the better part of three hours, with each of them telling the other of their life to that date. Ron explained about his desire to fly, the training he went through to get his wings, his terrible accident that resulted in his hospital stay. He talked fondly about his parents, how proud they were about him and how his Dad wanted him to take over the hardware shop only to be told that he wanted something that involved flying. He explained about the welcome home party where he had first met his wife. And he explained how his longing for a successful company had overrun his longing for a successful marriage and how it led him to the position in which he now finds himself, staying together with his wife to benefit the kids, sleeping in separate rooms, and finally his anticipated divorce. And there was his utter devotion to Condor. Not exactly the life he had envisioned for himself but as he grew older, it was the life that was given to him.

Natalie also opened up about her life. She was born in a little town outside of Chicago. Her mother was a single-mom for reasons that were still unclear. She had tried to broach the subject with her mother, but was always rebuffed. It was as though the remembrance by her mother was too painful to discuss. She was raised by her mother and her grandfather, both of whom worked. Her mother worked at night so as to be home during the day until she went to school, then she switched to a day job at a nursing home and worked enough hours to be home when she returned from school. Her grandfather worked in a factory making metal parts for automobiles. Both of them worked hard to give her the best they could.

Once old enough, Natalie did odd jobs like babysitting and so on in an attempt to save money for college. Her grades in school were good, so good as to earn her a scholarship to a college in New Jersey. While her mother was reluctant to see her go, it was a chance to make something of herself and with New York being so close and the opportunities that were there, it was finally agreed that she could move to New Jersey and attend school, provided they stayed in touch several times a week. So far it had worked out as planned.

When the waitress walked over and asked if everything was ok, Ron asked for the check, which was promptly delivered. He paid at the register, leaving a sizable tip on the table for the waitress first because of her excellent service, and second, for her realization that they wanted to be left alone to talk. The three hours was worth a little extra, thought Ron.

They had taken two cars that night and Ron said, "I'll follow you home to make sure you make it safely." Natalie protested that it was not necessary but Ron insisted and eventually she gave in. After parking next to her, Ron got out of his car to open her car door and walk her to her apartment building door.

Ron looked down at his watch and moaned that it had stopped. "What time is it?" he asked Natalie.

She smiled, grabbed his hand and said, "Later," as she pulled him through the door.

Chapter Thirty-One

Ron had never experienced anything like this before. It was nothing like two teenagers scrambling in the back seat to rid themselves of restrictive clothing and forget about everything their parents had ever told them. Nor was it the drunken rush to get this over and done before falling asleep. And it surely was nothing like "Honey, hurry up there is a show I want to watch."

No, it was more like two angels facing each other, their wings stretched out in front of them, the tips of which were touching the other's. It was like a hidden waterfall deep in the forest with mist that broke the streaming sunshine into strings of color that could only be seen and heard by those fortunate enough to be basking in its glory. It was like the only two people in the world, the Adam and Eve of their time, enjoying the goodness of their togetherness. It was like nothing else mattered.

And as the excitement grew the angels wings began searching and stroking, the waterfall picked up speed, the colors grew brighter and brighter and the silence grew louder and louder until it came to a crashing halt, accompanied by the breathless search for air and the desire for space. It was like a magical scene in the playhouse of the mind.

They lay there close to each other, as close as possible, each inch of skin searching for more skin to touch until it seemed like there was a melting of skin to make one body. Slowly they each recovered and realized what they had achieved. And Ron chuckled.

Natalie looked at him and asked "what is so funny?"

Ron turned his head and looked at her. "It reminds me of a joke," he said with a silly grin on his face.

"Well, let's hear it," was her response.

"A couple was lying in bed," he began, "and a Martian suddenly appeared at the foot of the bed. The man sat up and asked what he was doing there. The Martian answered that his home planet had sent their people out to other planets to study the reproductive practices of the people, the inhabitants, who lived on those different planets. His part of the project was earth and its inhabitants. Would they be willing to demonstrate their practices to him as he took notes?

The couple looked at each other and decided, for the sake of science, to demonstrate the human process to procreate the species. And saying that, they proceeded to indulge in first foreplay, then the reproductive intercourse itself. When they were done, the husband asked the Martian if he had enough material.

The Martian said he did, but also asked where the baby was that they had created. The husband responded that the baby would come in about nine months.

With that, the Martian, straight face and all, asked 'Then why the sudden rush at the end?'"

Natalie chuckled and with a fake grimace punched Ron on the shoulder. With that he started to get up.

"Where are you going?" she asked quietly.

"Thought I would head back to the office," he responded.

"No," she said like a child to a parent, "Please stay here with me."

Ron thought for perhaps half a second than laid back down, pulling the covers up over him. He slid his arm under her shoulders as she buried her head on his chest. They stayed that way as they fell asleep. A few hours later Ron woke up. Natalie appeared to be still sleeping soundly as he slid out of bed, put his clothes on and got ready to leave. Before leaving, however, he leaned over the bed and gave Natalie the slightest kiss on her forehead.

"See you in a couple of hours," she whispered in a tiny voice that filled the room with the love she was feeling.

Chapter Thirty-Two

The sun started to peek into Natalie's bedroom causing her to pull the covers over her head to block it out. She had nowhere to go this morning until she had to go to work at around noon. She glanced over to the other side of the bed where Ron had slept and thought about the night before. She smiled at the joy they had brought to each other, the feeling of togetherness, the delight in being able to bring pleasure to the other person, and the satisfaction of knowing that each enjoyed both the giving and the receiving. She rolled over and went back to sleep.

While hours seemed to pass it was only thirty minutes and her eyes opened again. Her eyes teared up as she replayed again the events of the night before. She realized that she had to share her happiness with someone.

"Mom," she thought. "I'll call Mom. She is the only one who would understand how I feel."

The phone rang twice before a quiet voice said "hello?"

"Hi Mom" Natalie said. How are you doing this morning?"

"Natalie, what are you calling me so early for. It's barely time for you to get up."

"I know, Mom, but I have to tell you something. Last night was wonderful."

There was silence on the other end of the phone. "What do you mean?" the concerned voice asked.

"Mom, we actually did it. We actually made love," she said with a lilt in her voice.

"You mean," the stern voice answered, "you got laid?"

"No, not like that. We made love, you know, the way you used to describe the feelings you and my father would feel as you physically showed each other how you felt about each other. We did the same thing, and it came naturally, not contrived, or set up, but like two natural beings who belonged together. Mom, it was wonderful and I now know what you must have felt when you experienced the same thing."

The moment of silence felt like an eternity.

"I have to meet this man, Natalie. He must be someone special for my daughter to fall in love with him, and I look forward to it."

Ron woke up out of a sound sleep with the bright sun coming in through the window. He jumped out of bed with the vigor he had not known for a while, started the coffee and headed for the shower. He had just finished when the coffee pot whistled its readiness to fill the cup and begin the day. Carrying the hot coffee to his desk, Ron began to read through the stack of papers for his final review. Every now and then, he would stand up, walk around the desk and think about the night before. He found it hard to comprehend the events of that night. And when he did, he smiled the likes of which he had not done in years. All was good in his mind.

He struggled not to think of his wife at home, but when he did it was more of a comparison than anything else. It had been such a long time since he and his wife had been intimate, it was almost a comparison between Natalie and nothing. And, as in such a case, Natalie always won.

Ron looked at his watch. Being Saturday morning, there were few people in the office and those that were there would probably only work half a day, and leave around noon. And that was fine as the proposal was almost ready to wrap up. All the input was in and most of it had been through the first review. All that was left was the final review and the assembly of the package. Margaret would over-see that process, with Natalie's help. Plane reservations had been made, contingency plans reviewed, people briefed, cars reserved and one person even took the trip as far as the computer giant's door. There would be no mistake on this one.

Ron kept plugging away at the stack of papers he needed to review and pretty much lost track of time. The coffee pot surrendered more and more of its precious commodity until it signaled its total displacement with a screeching squeal causing Ron to raise his head from his work. With a little chuckle, he got up from his chair, did a couple of knee bends to get his legs working, and walked back to the small kitchen to unplug the pot and accept its unconditional surrender. The morning had been very productive and he strolled back to his desk feeling pretty good about his progress so early in the day. A good start after a great night.

Chapter Thirty-Three

Ron was busy at his desk when he heard the familiar sounds of high heels clicking on the office floor. He looked up in time to see Natalie walk past the door to his office. She gave a little smile, waved ever so slightly, and continued on her journey to her cubicle for the day's chores. He followed the sound of the clicking till it stopped and the rolling of her chair took its place. He smiled as he envisioned the lithe body hiding beneath the free flowing material which mocked his curious eyes. He leaned back into his soft chair and thought about the night before and wondered how it all came together. "Never mind how it happened," he thought. "Just be happy it did happen."

And with that thought, and a bigger smile on his face, he went back to reviewing input for the proposal.

An hour went by and Ron stood up to stretch his legs and relax his eyes. He walked around the office, out the door and over to Natalie's desk. Though there was nobody in the office that Saturday morning, they both maintained their professional demeanor. After chatting a few minutes, Ron turned to head back to his office.

And it began. First, a little tingle in the fingers of his left hand, nothing to worry about as he shrugged the feeling off. Curiously, it started moving up his left arm, reaching the elbow in a couple of seconds and then moved upward. His legs began to feel like

180

rubber, unable to hold up his body and the whole room was spinning. He grabbed hold of the edge of a desk, trying to steady himself from falling. Nothing seemed to be working and he could feel himself slowly falling to the floor.

But he wasn't falling, he was collapsing.

Natalie noticed Ron shaking his left hand, then his arm. His knees were buckling and he tried to straighten up. But the legs gave out, and even trying to grab a desk didn't work and he collapsed into a heap on the floor. His body was shaking and spittle dripped from the side of his mouth. His head, where it had hit the floor, was bleeding from the blow and moans were coming from his mouth. His eyes were rolled back into his head and he was shaking worse now.

Natalie ran over to where Ron was lying and tried to help him. She soon realized that she was not prepared to do anything but the most remedial of tasks, none of which would solve the immediate situation. She ran to the phone.

"911, how can I help you?" the operator responded quickly.

"My boss just collapsed on the office floor and I need help immediately," she said quickly into the phone. "It looks like he had a heart attack. Please help."

"Easy, Miss. You don't have to yell. I can hear you perfectly. Where are you?"

Natalie gave all the information to the 911 operator. "Please hurry," she said. "I don't know how long he can last! Please, please hurry!"

"They are on the way, Miss. Please stay there to help direct them to your boss. They will be there shortly. Try to keep your boss comfortable and protect him from any further injury and we'll take it from there when we arrive."

It seemed like an eternity, but it was less than five minutes before the emergency team arrived. They were stationed at the airport in case of an aviation related emergencies so with lights flashing and sirens blaring, they had traversed the airport in quick time and jumped right into their protocol for someone who had suffered a heart attack.

The paramedics turned Ron on his side and checked in his mouth to make sure there was nothing obstructing his throat that would prevent breathing. They attached a heart monitor to his chest to keep track of the condition of the heart. The monitor showed wild swings of normalcy combined with erratic contractions as a result of the attack. They injected medicine to calm the heart down and restore its regular rhythm and they placed a respirator over his nose to ensure that oxygen was available. The respirator did not cover his mouth in case the stomach rebelled and vomited. When the initial prep was completed, they gently placed him on a rolling gurney and five of the paramedics escorted it to the waiting ambulance in front of the building. One paramedic stayed behind to gather information.

Natalie stood stunned as Ron was wheeled out of the office to the waiting vehicle outside. "Ma'm, can you tell me what happened?"

Natalie stumbled through the events leading up to the heart attack, trying mightily not to betray the real emotions she was feeling. Here was the man she had just learned to love, had just been with her in bed, who had been in her heart and mind since the night before. Now he was in severe danger of dying leaving her empty, angry, and alone. She told the paramedic all she could remember than excused herself saying there were phone calls she had to make. With that, she walked back to her desk, picked up the phone and dialed a number she had memorized but never expected to call.

"Hello," said the female voice on the other end.

"Mrs. Williams, this is Natalie from your husband's office. Your husband has had a heart attack, the paramedics have been here and are taking him to the hospital. You need to get there was soon as you can."

"Oh my God," exclaimed the rushing voice. "Is he all right? What happened? Where are they taking him?"

"He seemed to have survived the initial attack. The paramedics checked him out, gave him some medicine to settle the heart and attached a monitor to keep track of it. He was semi-conscious when leaving, moving in and out of consciousness. He probably has no idea what is going on. The paramedics said they were going to Newark General as that is the closest hospital so I would go there. If there is anything I can do to help, please call me at once. I will probably be awake all night so don't worry about waking me up. Your husband was like a good friend to me, so please keep me informed of his status. I'll stop by the hospital tomorrow and check on both you and him."

Lannis Williams slowly hung up the phone and peered down at the opened letter from the municipal county court house. Inside were the completed divorce papers which had stumbled their way through the legal system. She was now without the support of a husband, and based on Natalie's call, may soon be without the support of a long-time friend. Despite their differences, she still loved him and prayed for his well-being. She was worried about the children, how they would take the divorce and now the heart attack. Her mind ran through many scenarios as she rushed to get dressed and hurried to the hospital.

Natalie hung up the phone and for the first time since the incident, sat down and took a deep breath. A few minutes later, she again picked the phone.

"Hello," said the voice on the other end.

"Mamma, I need you to come right away. I need your help," she cried into the phone, tears flowing.

Chapter Thirty-Four

Natalie wondered around the office. A daze engulfed her body, the reality of the situation unable to penetrate the protective moat which encompassed her being. She floated from menial task to menial task, hoping they would make a difference, but none did. She sat and thought about her new-found relationship, what they had discovered and what now was wobbling on the edge of a cliff, ever threatening to fall off. She did manage to call Margaret, telling her what happened while trying to get a handle on the situation herself. Their discussion was curt, straight-forward, and unsupported of her fears. Margaret did say she was going to the hospital to see what she could find out and to be there for Mrs. Williams when she arrived. She had known her for a long time and wanted to be there in case she needed help She advised Natalie to call Dick and let him know, which she did.

The conversation with Dick was even shorter, nothing but the facts, no opinions of the cause of the stroke, no suppositions of what is to happen next, just the expected, "Oh my God" and the "I'm going to the hospital."

Natalie cleaned up Ron's desk, placing papers where they needed to be placed, arranging notes to be read, cleaning his coffee cup, and generally getting ready for the next day, not sure when that would be.

With that, she left the office and drove to her apartment, the daze clearing enough for her to safely get there. Once inside, she stood at the door and looked around her apartment, thinking that her life consisted of only all she could see, the furniture, the small kitchen table, the stereo set and the television set. Her diploma was properly displayed above the kitchen table, a testament to four years of hard work, which now seemed worthless. Her life now revolved around a man in the hospital, struggling between life and death, and holding control over her life's happiness. It had happened so fast, she had not realized what she had gotten herself into. As the realization slowly emerged from the depths of sorrow, she slowly sank to her knees and asked for help from above, from the very Lord she had forgotten over the years, yet the very One who could assist her.

The phone rang. She looked at it, afraid to answer it, afraid of what it may hold. She let it ring until it stopped. A couple of minutes later, the phone rang again. With the timidness of a mouse approaching the mousetrap cheese, she slowly picked up the receiver, put it to her ear and said, "Hello?"

"Natalie, are you alright?" said her mother on the other end. "Yes," said Natalie, "just thinking of things going on."

"I have made flight arrangements. The earliest I could get there is about noon tomorrow. Is that good for you?"

"Yes, Mom, I appreciate it and will pick you up at the airport and we'll go right to the hospital to see how things are going. I really thank you, Mom. You are always there for me and I want you to know that I

186

appreciate it. You're the best mom ever and look forward to seeing you tomorrow.

"Don't worry, dear, we will get through this together and things will be ok. Get some sleep, if possible. I'll call from the airport when we get ready to leave and give you the approximate time of arrival. We'll work on this together. Love you, dear."

"Love you too, Mom. Till tomorrow morning."

Chapter Thirty-Five

The night was not good for the mind. It rushed here and there, drifted into areas previously unknown, screamed past the realities of the day, and settled nowhere, hanging somewhere among the points of reality, the thoughts of the future, and the current situation. It was not a good night, but somehow Natalie got through it by getting up an hour before her usual time, drinking lots of coffee, watching the news and pondering on the various paths this day will take. As the time slipped by, she cleaned up, got dressed, and went to her car to pick up her mother.

Her Mom was there, on the sidewalk in front of the terminal, waving her arms to make sure her daughter saw her. Natalie smiled, her first in a while, and welcomed her Mom with open arms, a quiet kiss on the check and a subtle "thank you" in the ear. Her Mom pushed her back a little, looked her right in her eyes and said, "No thanks needed, that is what we women are made to do. So let's go to the hospital and see what has to be done."

Idle chatter about neighborhood friends filled the next ten minutes as they drove to the hospital. They parked the car and walked into the hospital lobby and straight to the welcome desk.

"Can you tell me on what floor the ICU is located. We have somebody there and want to visit them."

"Well, I can tell you that normally visitors are not permitted in the ICU rooms and usually have to wait outside to speak to a nurse or doctor. Only family are permitted inside the actual rooms. Are you part of the family?"

With a minimum of hesitation, Natalie's mother said, "This is his fiancé and she would like to see him. Isn't that right, *dear*?"

"Yes, please, I would like to see him," she responded, with a look and sound of despair.

The volunteer looked up at Natalie and with a sigh of resignation said "it is on the second floor, take a left out of the elevator. You'll have to check in at the nurse's desk and ask to see him. Good luck and God bless."

The elevator ride was smooth and short, they turned left, walked through a couple of arches and down some halls until the nurse's station loomed in front of them. Natalie walked up to the working nurse and asked what room Mr. Williams was in. The nurse, totally engaged in her work answered without looking up. "At the end of the hall on the left. There are others seated there also waiting for the doctor to return."

"Thank you" Natalie said, grabbed her mother's arm and started to walk down the hall to the end waiting area. Natalie looked to the end of the hall and saw Margaret and another woman who she suspected was Ron's wife. They were both seated quietly and looked very somber. As they approached, Margaret raised her head and stood up to greet Natalie.

"I had to come, Margaret, and find out his status. I could not just wait to hear," she continued. "Oh, this

189

is my mother," she said. "She came to help me get through this situation, hope you don't mind?"

"Not at all," said Margaret, "the more help the better. Hello, how do you do?"

"I am fine, thank you," replied Natalie's mom. "Hope you don't mind that I came. Natalie asked me to come and provide morale support for her. She has never been in a situation like this before and could use the help."

"Hi" said the other woman, "I'm Ron's wife. Thank you for coming. Natalie, we have never met but I thank you for calling me when you did. We got here just after the ambulance and were able to spend a couple of minutes with him as the nurses got him settled. Than we had to leave as the doctors began their examination. I appreciate your call."

"You're welcome," replied Natalie as she and her mother took a seat and waited for the medical report on Ron's condition.

The silence was deafening as the few minutes waiting seemed like hours until the door to Ron's room opened and the doctor walked out. He looked as the four women waiting for him stood up, anxious to hear some good words.

"Mrs. Williams?" he asked, not knowing who was who.

"I'm Mrs. Williams," she said quickly, moving to shake the doctor's hand. "How is he?"

"Your husband has had a strong heart attack, the cause of which is still unknown. It could be some kind of medical condition or could have been caused by some outside forces like pressure at work, social conditions, home conditions, or a combination of things that his heart was unable to take and took this action to tell him, *enough is enough*. We don't know until we do more tests to see if there are any medical conditions that could have caused this. While we gather the information, we have sedated him, which will probably keep him unresponsive to anything you say to him. We also have hooked him up to a respirator to ensure his breathing. We have already done some tests and are awaiting the results and will be doing some more this afternoon. I will be in contact with you later this afternoon with whatever new information I have."

"As for the moment, you can go visit him for a couple of minutes, but as I said, don't expect a response. I would go about your business as best you can and rest assured he is in very good hands. And please contact me should you have any questions before the report," he said, handing them a card with his name and number on it. He turned and walked away before any of the women could respond.

"Thank you." said Ron's wife. "Margaret, would you please come in with me. I could use your arm to hold onto."

"Absolutely," said Margaret as she helped open the door to Ron's room.

Natalie and her mom sat back down on their chairs and tried to process what the doctor had said. They were trying to read between the lines, to understand not only what was said, but was not said. It was not an easy task. There was no mention of Ron's actual condition. Was he critical, or stable, was he going to be all right, was his thought process going to be affected, his speech, his physical movement? None of that was addressed. Perhaps the answers were not known and won't be known until the test results are studied. But knowing that did not allay the fears that accompany situations of this type. Fear would always raise its ugly head when the unknown held sway. And this was one of those instances.

Ron's door opened and the two women slowly stepped out. Margaret was holding the other woman's shoulders, steadying her as she stumbled to her seat, weeping silently, the tissue wiping the tears away from her eyes.

"Margaret," said Ron's wife, "please take me home. I need some time for this, but have some tea with me when we get there before leaving. I need someone to talk to and the kids won't understand."

"Of course," said Margaret. "But wait here, I'm going to get a wheelchair for you. I'm sure they won't mind considering the circumstances." She stood up and went to the nurse's station, returning in a couple of minutes with a wheelchair. As she helped Lannis to the wheelchair, she said to Natalie she would let her know if and when she heard anything. Natalie nodded and watched them go down the hall.

When they turned the corner and were out of sight Natalie stood up and started to walk toward Ron's door. She looked back as her mother followed behind, struggling a little bit with a sore knee. They slowly and quietly opened the door, peered around from the outside, than slowly walked in.

There, straight ahead, was Ron lying in bed. His eyes were closed, a sheet and blanked tucked under his chin, his arms under the covers except the one punctured by the IV. A stand behind the bed held the bag of medicine meandering its way through the plastic tube into the arm, medicine apparently to keep him sedated.

A respirator stood on its metal stand, another plastic tube attached to it, the other end disappearing into Ron's nose and down to his lungs. A pressure gauge on the respirator displayed how much oxygen was being fed into the lungs, indicting how much he was breathing on his own and how much the respirator was acting as his lungs. The gauge needle was in the yellow area meaning both the lungs and the machine were sharing the duties. This was not ideal, but better than the red area which would mean he was not breathing at all and the machine was keeping him alive. That would be bad.

Natalie moved to the side of the bed and touched his uncovered hand. There was no response, but the hand was warm, which was a good sign. She stroked it a little and talked to him slowly and softly, telling him she was there should he awake and remember. Even if he did not remember, it did her good knowing she talked to him for a while.

Natalie's mom moved closer to the end of the bed and stared intently at Ron's face. Memories of long ago and faraway places raced through her mind and she gasped with the realization.

"Natalie, let's go now. That's enough for one time. We will come back tomorrow and perhaps things will be better."

Natalie nodded her consent, kissed Ron's hand, and quietly left the room with her mother. They drove back to her place in silence and quickly opened a bottle of wine. It was gone in a flash, and thank goodness, another one appeared. Sleep was a welcome respite.

Chapter Thirty-Six

The attacking rays of the rising orb flung themselves against the shuttered drapes, sneaking around, through, and under them reaching the closed eyelids till finally there was no more resistance. Ingrid opened her eyes and looked around. The splattered light filled the bedroom like a van Gogh painting, keeping her eyes moving from wall to wall, or in this case, print to print.

Her night had been restless once the effects of the wine had worn off. She thought about her daughter and the man in the hospital, a man she had not seen in decades thinking he was dead, a man who had taught her to live, and to love. But her thoughts were not kind. The one word which kept popping up was "violate". He had violated Natalie, whether it was consensual or not, whether it was knowingly or not, and whether it was intentional or not. And equally important as the physical violation was the taking away the thrill of the first love and the dreams of what the future would hold. This would all be gone once their relationship was revealed in whatever way. What could she do to prevent the hurt that would come to Natalie? How should she tell the truth without destroying the young spirit which defined Natalie? What should she do had been the subject of all her nightly ponderings. And among those thoughts, the remembrance of her first love had clawed its way up the ladder of human emotions. And a knowing smile graced her lips as the sparkle returned to her eyes.

The answer had been slow in arriving. It had survived the countless questions that it raised. It would free Natalie from the curse of the past and open the door to the future. Yes, there would initially be pain and sorrow, but that would wane over time. She had decided on the answer, an answer that would unlock the dreams of the future for Natalie.

"Good morning," she said, walking into the kitchen.

"Hi Mom, just making some coffee and scrambled eggs. Want some?"

"Just coffee, black please," she answered. "What time do you want to go to the hospital?"

Natalie said "around noon should be a good time. Should be a little quiet by then and perhaps some test results will be available."

"Sounds like a plan," Ingrid responded sitting down at the kitchen table. Natalie joined her and they chatted for the next couple of hours till it was time to get ready and go to the hospital.

"Mom," Natalie asked again for the umpteenth time. "Why did you not ever marry after you left Germany and moved to Chicago with Grandpa?

Ingrid had answered this questions several times over the years. She had managed to brush aside the question when Natalie was a young girl by saying that the knight on his white horse had not yet arrived. Several times when she was being picked up for a date, Natalie would look outside and ask the man where his white horse was. Ingrid had laughed to herself and thought, "Not yet," shrugging her shoulders to Natalie as if to say "I don't know".

As the years had passed, the question arose less frequently as though Natalie had given up on looking for the white horse and resigned herself to the family of three, her, her mother, and her grandpa. Not a bad arrangement, but something was missing.

The traffic was light on the way to the hospital and arriving there they were able to find a parking space pretty close to the entrance. Entering the lobby, they nodded to the volunteer at the welcome desk and continued walking to the elevators. At the second floor, they exited, turned left and again walked the halls till they got to the small waiting area by Ron's room. His door was shut, but they could hear some movement inside. They decided to wait till whoever was inside was done with what they were doing and came out. Perhaps they could get an update at that time.

A nurse came out of the room and they asked her if there was any information she could share. She said" he is resting well. His breathing is a little labored so we are watching that. As for test results, you'll have to wait till the doctor visits again after he finishes his initial rounds." Looking at her watch, she continued. "About half an hour."

"Can we see him?" Natalie asked. "Yes," said the nurse, "but please be quiet."

As the nurse turned and walked back to her station, Natalie and her mom entered Ron's room. It was pretty much the same as the day before. The IV was still in place and almost full, revealing it had just been hung. The respirator was still hooked up although the gauge was much more into the yellow, verifying the breathing issue the nurse had explained. The heart monitor was still hooked up. A clean blanket had been placed on the bed and tucked in at the bottom allowing for easy movement of the arms if there was a need. All in all, the scene pretty much mirrored yesterday's. After a while, they went back to their seats in the hallway to wait for the doctor.

A couple of minutes went by and Natalie said she had to use the restroom and would be back shortly. Watching her leave, Ingrid hesitated for a moment than quietly walked to Ron's door, opened it, and entered. She had thought this idea through and through but now when it was time to execute it, she hesitated. But her conviction soon won out.

She moved to the respirator and flipped the off button. The humming sound of the machine abruptly stopped and there was a slight jerk of Ron's body as the artificial oxygen ceased to flow. The heart monitor began acting inconsistently showing the heart was reacting to the lack of oxygen. Ron's lungs tried gasping for air, but they were too weak to inhale enough to sustain the body. In two minutes, the heart monitor flat-lined and Ingrid could hear the alert sound coming from the nurse's station.

Bending over Ron's head, she whispered in his ear "I love you, still."

She reached into her pocket and pulled out an old picture and held it tightly while reaching into the other pocket and retrieving a small derringer pistol which she always carried for self defense. "I'll be right there with you, Ron. Wait for me."

With that, she put the pistol to her temple and pulled the trigger.

Nurses scrambled from their stations when they heard the alarm from the heart monitor, hesitating only momentarily upon hearing the sound of the pistol. Racing to Ron's room, they opened the door and found the tragedy inside. One nurse ran to Ron's side to check on him, but stood back and shook her head in response to the question. Two other nurses moved to Ingrid but in seeing the wound, realized there was nothing they could do.

Natalie burst into the room brushing aside the nurses. She quickly checked Ron and realized he was gone. Seeing her mother on the floor, she rapidly moved to her. Natalie saw the little pistol on the floor and the blood flowing from the head. There was no denying the intended result of the gunshot.

Natalie glanced at the other hand. It held a picture of a young man and woman standing underneath a sign that read "Bad Durkheim Weinfest". The man in the picture was dressed in an old Army uniform, the woman clothed in a traditional German dress. She turned the picture over and read

Ron and Ingrid
1949

Natalie fell to her knees and wept uncontrollably, as did the tiny heart in her womb.

Epilogue

She buried them there, side by side
As they should have able to live their lives But
the world events just wouldn't let them do it

She knelt to pray for both of them
The Father, the Son, and the Holy Spirit
And asked the Lord to hold them tight forever

Hallelujah

About the Author

CARL MESSINGER is a decorated Vietnam veteran and retired Army officer who started writing in the early 80's while living in Germany. Traveling throughout Europe, he saw the opportunity to write travel articles and at the same time, deduct the expenses incurred while traveling as business expenses. He began taking notes during his travels and submitting the resultant articles to various travel magazines. After about six months, his first article about Heidelberg was accepted for publication by World Traveling magazine. Others soon followed.

Returning from Germany, Carl, an amateur thespian settled in the Philadelphia area. Combining his knowledge of the theater and his desire to write, he started covering the local theater scene for several newspapers as a free-lance critic. Later on, he moved to Northern Virginia and continued his coverage of local theaters, including the famed Folger's Theater in Washington D.C.

Moving to Arizona, Carl's first novel, *Tent City: An Arizona Tragedy* was published and is currently available on Amazon. This is Carl's second novel and the first in a series of novels detailing the life and consequences of the Williams family. The second book of the series is currently under construction.

CPSIA information can be obtained
at www.ICGtesting.com
Printed in the USA
LVHW050252050720
659748LV00004B/243

9 780578 675206